THE DEVIL'S ROUNDUP

Other Five Star Titles
by Will Cook:

The Rain Tree (1996)
A Saga of Texas: Until Day Breaks (1999)
A Saga of Texas: Until Shadows Fall (2000)
A Saga of Texas: Until Darkness Disappears (2001)

Other Five Star Titles
Edited by Bill Pronzini:

Under the Burning Sun by H.A. DeRosso (1997)
Renegade River by Giff Cheshire (1998)
Riders of the Shadowlands by H.A. DeRosso (1999)
Heading West by Noel M. Loomis (1999)
Tracks in the Sand by H.A. DeRosso (2001)

Other Five Star Titles
by Bill Pronzini:

All the Long Years (2001)

THE DEVIL'S ROUNDUP

A WESTERN QUINTET

WILL COOK

EDITED BY

BILL PRONZINI

Five Star • Waterville, Maine

Five Star First Edition Western Series.

Published in 2002 in conjunction with Golden West Literary Agency.

Cover design by Thorndike Press Staff.

Set in 11 pt. Plantin by Rick Gundberg.

Printed in the United States on permanent paper.

Library of Congress Cataloging-in-Publication Data

Cook, Will.
    The Devil's roundup : a western quintet / by Will Cook ; edited by Bill Pronzini.—1st ed.
        p. cm.
    Contents: The barbed wire war—The big kill—The range that hell forgot—The Devil's roundup—The sheriff's lady.
    ISBN 0-7862-3534-9 (hc : alk. paper)
    1. Western stories. I. Pronzini, Bill. II. Title.
PS3553.O5547 D48 2002
    813'.54—dc21   2002024356

TABLE OF CONTENTS

FOREWORD

Will Cook's relatively short life—he died of a heart attack in 1964, at age forty-two—was packed with more action and adventure than the lives of any of his fictional characters. Born in Indiana in 1921, he ran away from home at sixteen to join the U.S. Cavalry. He became disillusioned with that branch of the service when horses were eliminated as a result of mechanization, and transferred to the U.S. Army Air Force. During World War II, he served as a pilot in the South Pacific. In the post-war years he flew as a bush pilot in Alaska, and later worked as a deputy sheriff in northern California. He had a passion for sports cars and sports car racing, and for boats. At the time of his death, he was engaged in building a sailing vessel in which he intended to sail to Polynesia with his family.

Like his life, Cook's writing career was relatively short and intensely pursued. He began producing fiction in 1951; his first three published short stories appeared in the same month, March of 1953, in Western pulp magazines, and his first novel, *Frontier Feud*, was a Popular Library paperback original the following year. Between 1951 and 1964, he published sixty short stories and novelettes (all but a handful of these in the period 1953–1955) and fifty novels under his own name and the pseudonyms James Keene, Wade Everett, and Frank Peace. Several other novels, completed prior to his death, appeared posthumously.

Nearly all of Cook's fictional output is traditional or historical Westerns. He wrote often and well of the U.S. Cavalry and its encounters with various Native American tribes, most notably in a series of related stories. Of these, "Comanche Captives" first appeared in serial form in *The Saturday Evening Post* (3/14/59–4/25/59) and was later filmed by John Ford as *Two Rode Together* (Columbia, 1961). These stories have since been published in an integrated trilogy, as intended by the author: *A Saga of Texas Book One: Until Day Breaks* (Five Star Westerns, 1999), *A Saga of Texas Book Two: Until Shadows Fall* (Five Star Westerns, 2000), and *A Saga of Texas Book Three: Until Darkness Disappears* (Five Star Westerns, 2001). Much of Will Cook's other Western fiction dealt with such standard Western themes as range wars, cattle rustling, and frontier law enforcement. Among the best of these are *Seven for Vengeance* (Random House, 1958) by James Keene, a tense suspense tale involving the disparate members of a man-hunting posse, and *The Rain Tree* (Five Star Westerns, 1996) that effectively chronicles the lives and rainmaking efforts of settlers on the arid Western plains. Cook was equally adept at the Western historical novel as evidenced by *Sabrina Kane* (Dodd, Mead, 1956), vividly set in frontier Illinois in 1811; *Elizabeth, by Name* (Dodd, Mead, 1958), a sharply realistic romance of the Texas plains in the 1870s; and *The Breakthrough* (Macmillan, 1963), a powerful study of the hardships and bigotry faced by a returning Native American veteran of the First World War.

In both novels and short stories, Cook often linked otherwise independent tales through the use of recurring characters. The five short novels in these pages are a good example. Written early in his career, all five appeared between March, 1953 and February, 1954. The first, "The Barb Wire War,"

8

was his fourth published story. Two initially appeared under the pseudonym Frank Peace, a borrowing of the name of the protagonist of *Trouble Shooter*, a 1937 novel by Ernest Haycox, a writer who Cook greatly admired.

This frontier quintet shares a common northern Texas cattle country setting and records the interrelated lives of their protagonists over a span of some twenty years, beginning in 1877. In "The Barb Wire War" tough young visionary Wes Cardigan struggles to introduce shorthorn cattle and barb-wire fencing to a region stubbornly controlled by longhorn breeders. John Saber, an old friend of Cardigan's and a federal marshal, is brought in to investigate rustling in "The Big Kill," and stays on to marry and become a wealthy and powerful cattle baron himself. Willie Kerry, a young cowhand with a small ranch, finds love at a price in "The Range that Hell Forgot," and is later appointed interim sheriff of the nearby town, Hondo, in order to quell trouble with desert dwellers in "The Sheriff's Lady." Phil Stalker, an inexperienced drifter who dreams of being a lawyer, makes his first appearance in "The Devil's Roundup," in which he uncovers the solution to a case of brand blotting. Like Saber, he then marries and settles in the community.

The lives, loves, trials, and triumphs of these four men are presented with raw realism and simple understanding. As Western fiction authority R.E. Briney has noted, a hallmark of Cook's fiction is his "compassion for his characters who must be able to survive in a wild and violent land. His protagonists make mistakes, hurt people they care for, and sometimes succumb to ignoble impulses, but this all provides an added dimension to the artistry of his work."

If these early tales are less polished, less fully realized, than the author's later fiction, they nonetheless contain all the elements of story, character, and background that make

Will Cook's body of work among the most entertaining published during the Western renaissance of the 'Fifties and 'Sixties, and among the most developmentally significant as well.

Bill Pronzini
Petaluma, California

THE BARB WIRE WAR

I

He stood in the vestibule, bracing himself against the lurch of the coach as the train slowed to enter town. He took a long drag on his cigar and spun it away from him, the red end fashioning a brief dance in the night. The lights of a section gang's shanty flashed by, and the sharp odor of the Hondo loading pens faded away. Up ahead, the engineer applied the brakes, gently at first, then with a determination that wrung squeals from the tracks with a sharp banging of loose couplings.

Wes Cardigan thrust his head past the edge of the coach as the station lights spread into yellow squares of lamplight. The train stopped with a last futile jerk that threw him shoulder-first against the door frame. He cursed mildly, and lifted his valise to step down to the cinder platform. Ahead of him, the engine puffed and snorted, its glowing firebox sending wavering fingers of light against the side of the baggage depot. The agent shouted to someone in the mail car, and Cardigan gave him a quick glance, pausing by the telegrapher's window to watch him rattle a key to a mute length of wire. He tapped lightly on the window, and the man shoved his green eyeshade to the back of his head, and turned to the window. He grinned as he recognized Cardigan. The window

11

squealed, stuck, and squealed again, as he pushed it open. He put his head close to Cardigan and spoke softly: "Just got it in, Wes. The shipment left Council Bluff last night."

Cardigan nodded, and turned toward the darkened end of the platform, his long-legged stride carrying him toward the red dot that glowed and died against the side of the station. He halted alongside the man, thumbed his hat to the back of his head. He brushed his full roan mustache with a forefinger, and stuck a fresh cigar between his thin lips.

"Well?" Cardigan asked impatiently. "Did you get all of them dug?"

Turkey Jack shoved himself away from the wall, hooked a thumb in his sagging gun belt. "Yep," he said, and his wrinkled old face creased in a lopsided grin. "There was some folks around here that said you wouldn't come back after what happened last month."

Cardigan fumbled through his pockets for a match. Turkey Jack wiped one alight, holding it before him. Cardigan bent a little to puff his smoke, and the brief flare played against his pale eyes and the harsh angles of his young face. His hair glinted a light, reddish brown; the full mustache hid his upper lip. "Tonight's the night, ain't it?" he asked, an odd stirring in his usually calm voice.

"Still aimin' to defy the old buzzard?"

Cardigan studied the red tip of his cigar and said: "What do you think?"

Turkey Jack grunted softly. "Figured you would, so I brought this along for you." He handed the curled shell belt and holstered gun to Cardigan.

The tall man's mouth pulled into a severe line, and he shook his head slowly from side to side.

Turkey Jack quickly thrust the gun at him and said tightly: "Don't be a damned fool about this thing, Wes. The time for talkin' is past. You ain't wore it for five years, but times have changed around here."

Cardigan studied his foreman in the half light and took the gun, brushing his coat tail aside to buckle the cartridge-laden belt around his waist. He raised his head, looking past the depot along the length of Comanche Street. Fragments of lamplight dotted the loose dust, and a cluster of horses made a dark knot in front of the Alamo House. Two doors down, the swinging doors of Keno Charlie's saloon waved idly, and three men paused on the darkened gallery to converse in low tones.

Turkey Jack observed Cardigan's attention and muttered: "Yeah, Ackerman rode in early . . . him and his two gunnies."

A high-sided lumber wagon rumbled the length of the street, made a ponderous U-turn, and halted before Rutherford's store. Cardigan brushed his mustache, and Turkey Jack added: "Second family this month. Word sure gets around."

"They're no problem," Cardigan said impatiently, and slipped the .44 American from the holster. He broke it open, glanced at the unfired primers, and closed it with a vicious snap. "Where are they now?"

Turkey Jack took off his hat, brushed at the thinning gray hair. "Miles Straight and Pete Kerry are waiting for us at the Alamo House bar." He took Cardigan's sleeve and added hotly: "Let me go alone, Wes. I can take Bitter Creek off your hands for you, permanent."

Cardigan gave him a long glance, and Turkey Jack lowered his eyes to study his boots. The silence hung between them like a palpable thing, like some obscene scribbling on a backyard fence. Cardigan cleared his throat, said softly— "Let's get at it then and get it over with."—and cut behind the depot.

They walked toward Comanche Street in silence, Turkey
Jack a little to Cardigan's right rear, his bone-handled Colt
beating against his skinny thigh. They struck the boardwalk
with a sharp drumming of boots, and Cardigan paused to
study the team tied before Harry Rutherford's store. One of
the horses, a big Clydesdale, stamped a forefoot impatiently.
Cardigan glanced through the open door. Rutherford raised
his head, and surprise washed across his narrow face. He
smothered it quickly, motioned to Cardigan with his hand.

The tall man stepped past a pile of stacked boxes,
threaded his way past the hanging harness, and leaned on the
counter beside the big homesteader and his family. He
studied Cardigan with a level neutrality, glanced at the tied-
down gun, and shifted his eyes.

Cardigan swung his eyes to the women. One was middle-
aged, her round face criss-crossed with the lines of hard work.
He sucked in his breath silently as the other, a young woman,
turned away from the notions counter. He stared at her for a
full ten seconds before he realized it, then dropped his eyes
quickly, the picture burning, sharp and clear, in his brain.
She was tall, and her pale gold hair fell in loosely braided
ropes against her gently curving shoulders. Her eyes, when
she had glanced at him, were a deep blue, and the full mouth
pulled into a faint smile. There was an aura of friendliness
about her, an open-handed trust in life that pushed aside all
pretense and convention. *That woman is fire,* Cardigan
thought. *She'd be worth a man's time fighting for.*

He brushed his mustache with his finger, raised his head
as Rutherford's whining voice came to him. "Saw you pass,
Wesley, and I just wondered if you'd care to settle up."

Turkey Jack growled something under his breath, and
Cardigan's brow wrinkled into a frown. "This isn't the first of
the month, Harry."

Rutherford spread his hands in the time-worn gesture. "I know that, Wesley, but some of the Sunrise boys have been spending right free. I sorta like to keep things straight."

Turkey Jack pushed against the big homesteader, trying to get past, and Cardigan stopped him with a slight movement of his hand. He was aware that he was being watched, and he caught sight of a young man, blond like the girl, edging his way into the group.

"Let's see the bill," Cardigan said, and touched a match to his dead cigar.

Rutherford rustled papers under the counter, and slid the sheet across to him. Cardigan glanced at it and said thinly—"This is less than usual, Harry."—and let the statement lay.

Rutherford ran a finger around a collar that had suddenly grown too tight. "To tell you the truth, Wesley, some folks didn't know if you was coming back or not. Ain't many that would have blamed you . . . with Amos Ackerman and his gun hands on your tail. He's in town, and Moose Dugan and Bitter Creek are trailing along behind him." He added lamely: "Fella's got to look out for his own interests."

"Maybe you think I won't be alive to pay this by the first of the month." Cardigan picked up the bill and waved it in the storekeeper's face.

"Now, Wesley," Rutherford whined. "I'm just bein' careful, that's all. Moose Dugan has been after you ever since you and him had that fight over Julia Ackerman. He's been after you to pack a gun . . . and now you're carryin' one. You got Amos Ackerman down on you for bringing in them damned blooded Hereford bulls." Rutherford shook his head sadly, and added: "If it don't make no difference to you, pay the bill now."

Cardigan glared at him until he dropped his eyes. He dug into his pocket and counted out a hundred and thirty-one dollars. He scrawled his name across the bill, added paid in full, and the date, August 10, 1877. There was a hard, dancing light in his gray eyes as he shoved it toward Rutherford. He said: "That's the last dime I'll ever spend in your damn' store!"

The little man bristled at the affront, and his lips tightened. "You may not act so damned high and mighty when Ackerman gets through with you. You been cuttin' a big patch in this country, but you sure bit off more than you can chew now . . . and I'm glad to see it come!"

The talk bit into Cardigan. He reached a lazy arm across the counter and pulled the little man against him. The cigar jerked as he spoke. "Harry, my father made you. I was just a kid, but I remember you coming into this country with your bottom peeking out the holes in your pants and not two dollars to rattle in your pockets." He lowered his voice and added ominously: "Maybe it would be better if you sold out." He released his grip, allowing the man to sag back. He turned as the blonde girl pushed past the big homesteader and placed both hands flatly against his chest.

Her eyes were pools of flickering temper. When the older man took her arm, she shook it off and said caustically: "Aren't you afraid you'll strain your muscles picking on a man half your size? That's the way a cattleman operates, isn't it, shooting and burning and fighting people too small and weak to fight back?"

Cardigan felt the warmth of her hands through his silk shirt, and his heart hammered oddly. He took her gently by the waist and said: "I have enough trouble for tonight, but I'll discuss that further . . . later." He smiled at her, and her eyes widened at the change in his face. She saw neither harshness nor cruelty there. It was a young face, and there was no apology in his manner as he lifted her aside so he could walk

16

out. That one thing told her what he was, a man who moved things that stood in his way, one who did so relentlessly, without passion or hate. Cardigan tipped his hat to her and strode from the store, Turkey Jack following obediently a few paces to the rear.

Wes Cardigan paused on the boardwalk, and Turkey Jack muttered: "That's the first one, but there'll be others. You can already feel the change. Folks figure the ship's sinkin' and are transferrin' over to the Ackerman crowd." He felt Cardigan stiffen, glanced at the tall man as the door of the Alamo House opened and a slim, long-legged girl stepped into the dust and crossed the street. Turkey Jack growled softly: "Don't get your hackles up. She likes you."

Cardigan cursed to himself, wondering why Julia Ackerman made him feel uneasy and defensive when they were together. She ducked under the hitch rail and stopped in the half light of Rutherford's store. She was shapely, the curve of her hips and long thighs filling her blue jeans. Her small breasts rose and fell with her breathing, as she watched him with her dark, unreadable eyes. When he didn't speak, she moved close to him and touched him.

"You don't seem glad to see me, Wes," she said softly. "I missed you something awful."

Cardigan shook his head, saying: "Not now, Julia. It's too late."

"Wes," her voice was pleading. "Don't go over there. Back down this once, and let things stand as they are. Bitter Creek is with Father, and I don't want anything to happen to either of you."

"It's too late," he repeated. "I've bought the bulls, and I'm going through with it." The thought of impending trouble whetted his appetite. "Come with me. If Bitter Creek gets proddy, I'll give you his ears for a present."

"No!" she said hotly, then in a softer voice: "Don't be a fool, Wes. Dad is ready to fight to the last man over this. What you're doing is madness." She gripped his sleeves, laid her head imploringly against him. "Remember how it was with us, Wes. Don't destroy it now for . . . for this foolishness. Dad forgave you when you let the homesteaders on your place, but he won't for this."

The blonde girl came out of Rutherford's, paused a moment to study him, and mounted the wheel of the heavy wagon. Cardigan stiffened and pushed Julia away from him, feeling strangely ill at ease at having been caught with Julia pressed against him. He raised his eyes and found the girl watching him, and somehow he felt that she would hold this against him. He stroked his mustache and said: "Julia, we've known each other for twelve years . . . ever since your father moved to this country. We've had a lot of fun together, you and I, but I never said that I loved you, and, if I ever did or said anything to make you believe that I did . . . well, I'm sorry."

She backed a step away from him, her mouth a round O.

Turkey Jack scowled, and shifted his big feet.

Julia's voice was a small, tight sound in the night. "What are you trying to say, Wes?"

"That this night may well be the end of our friendship."

"It will never end . . . not as far as I'm concerned," Julia said firmly.

Cardigan shook his head. "When that barbed wire goes up between the Sunrise and Leaning Seven, there will be no more you and me. It will be you with your people, and me. . . ." He let the rest trail off into nothingness. He glanced at the Alamo House, ablaze with lights. He touched her arm, and asked: "Sure you don't want to come?"

She shook her head. "Promise me one thing, Wes . . . don't hurt Bitter Creek."

He made no attempt to mask his surprise. He stepped in closer to grip her shoulders. "What is this?" His tone was sharp. "Ever since we were kids, it's been there between us . . . this warped, half-crazy killer. He's always held a fascination for you, hasn't he?" He stopped. "No! I won't promise you that. I'll kill him if he moves an eyelash."

"No, Wes!" Her face was twisted in fright. "If you never promise me anything else . . . promise me that!"

Cardigan glanced at Turkey Jack, and the old man nodded imperceptibly. Cardigan let out a long breath and said—"All right."—and moved away to cross the street.

II

Amos Ackerman made a thin, high shape against the west wall of the room, as he watched Cardigan through narrowed eyes. Pete Kerry and his two lank, half-grown sons sat hunkered in their chairs, Pete nursing his pipe with a slow, puffing patience. Turkey Jack left Cardigan to stand by Miles Straight and his four boys, Straight's heavy body blocking him from Moose Dugan's view, but allowing him to cover Bitter Creek. Cardigan watched Turkey Jack and Bitter Creek, feeling the hatred pass between them, but not understanding it. It was something that had happened before his time, something that had occurred before Amos Ackerman moved to north Texas when Turkey Jack had then been the *segundo* of Ackerman's southern empire. Turkey Jack and the small gunman continued to exchange thinly veiled glances, as Bitter Creek toyed with the huge, silver buckle on his gun belt. Moose Dugan leaned his bulk toward the scowling Ackerman, whispered something to him, and Ackerman dropped his eyes quickly to Cardigan's sagging gun.

The old man shoved his gaunt body away from the wall with his elbows, and said: "It's been a month since we've been together in this room. The last time changed things for all of us, and tonight we're gonna find out which way it changed." He pointed a bony finger at Cardigan. "You . . . you stood right where you're standin' now, and told me you was gonna fence your place. You gave me your reasons, and I gave mine against it. I'll give 'em to you again. Longhorn cattle has been good enough for Texas for thirty years, and they're good enough now. Them twenty white-faced bulls you bought will ruin Texas and every cow in it. They can't live on the open range like a longhorn. A critter has to be tough and wild to survive, and they don't need no barbed-wire fences, either."

Cardigan smiled thinly, and slid his low voice in. "You forgot to mention that there's more profit in the shorthorn. They'll dress out three hundred pounds heavier at two years old, and the meat ain't so damned tough and stringy you can't cut it with an axe. The railroad is here now, and long cattle drives are a thing of the past. It used to cost you a dollar a head, and a few men's lives to drive to Abilene. Now, you can ship from here, and the beef goes direct to Chicago."

The old man's face flooded, and Cardigan felt pleased at this sign of his rising temper. "That sounds pretty, Cardigan . . . but you ain't told it all."

"These men know without being told," Cardigan stated.

"Those blasted shorthorns mean fences . . . barbed-wire fences!" The old man took hold of his temper, and his voice went low and wicked. "Cardigan, you stood right here last month and told me to my face that you was goin' East to buy wire. I told you I'd kill you if you brought back a foot of it." Bitter Creek shifted his feet and glanced between Cardigan and Turkey Jack. Pete Kerry cleared his throat, the sound tearing the room's silence.

Cardigan took one step forward and brushed his coat away from the cedar butt of his Smith and Wesson. "I came back, Ackerman . . . and the wire is on its way. There's enough of it to fence ten thousand acres. Enough to keep your herd out of Mix Cañon and the upper range beyond. Whatever arrangement you had before for winter graze in my high country is off now. I'm going to breed a herd of shorthorns, and I didn't pay a good price for them bulls to strengthen your herd." He watched the old man stiffen. "You're surprised, ain't you? You figured the Ackerman threat would stop me . . . well, it didn't!" Cardigan used his voice like a whip. "You're old and slow . . . bluff and brag. I'm wearing a gun tonight, and you know that you won't reach into that shoulder holster for yours . . . you don't want to die."

Pete Kerry sucked in his breath sharply, and Turkey Jack stepped away from the wall to face Bitter Creek squarely. He let his fingers curl around the bone handle of his cap-and-ball Colt. Bitter Creek watched him with a frozen-faced alertness. Moose Dugan growled something in his throat, and Miles Straight turned toward him, sliding his hand under his coat.

They stood there, frozen, with only the sawing of their breathing breaking the silence.

Cardigan spoke softly. "Give the word, old man, and we'll lace you with lead, you and your two hired guns."

Amos Ackerman licked his dry lips, and sagged against the wall. He spoke to Kerry and Straight. "All right. You've thrown in with this nester-lover. When I finish with him, I'm goin' to run you clean out of the state of Texas."

Pete Kerry's older boy spoke up. "You ain't runnin' him out tonight, loudmouth."

21

Ackerman swiveled his head to glare at him. "I'll remember you, sonny."

"Do that," the boy said, and grinned at him.

Amos Ackerman turned to Cardigan. "Your father and I always got along fine, ever since I moved to this country. I never thought I'd live to see the day when wire blocked the Leaning Seven from Sunrise graze." He drew a ragged breath. "I said nothing when you cut up that land above Devil's Gorge for these nesters. I made no move to drive them out."

"That's lucky for you," Cardigan said, "because I'd have killed you for it."

The old man's eyes flickered. "Your dad would turn over in his grave if he knew you was givin' away land to these hoemen. He hated a nester."

"You're wrong," Cardigan insisted. "He never disliked an honest man."

Amos Ackerman made a motion toward Turkey Jack and Straight. "Right now you have me on the hip, but I'm givin' you a flat warnin' here and now. If that wire goes up, I'll run you into a grave, if I have to hire every gun in Texas."

Cardigan felt his temper slip, and he paced the length of the room to pause before Amos Ackerman. He tapped his words out on the old man's bony chest with a stiff finger. "You've tried to ram your brand of rule down our throats ever since you moved here. You tried to make the Leaning Seven, your brand, a thing to fear, and I say it's come to an end. The land doesn't belong to you. It doesn't belong to me. It belongs to the government, and it's free to settle on."

"A man takes what he wants, and holds it if he can!" Amos shouted.

"That's right," Cardigan agreed. "That's how you got yours . . . drove the people off with rifle and burning torch, but you weren't strong enough to take Sunrise. I don't want to war with you, but if you touch one post, one strand of wire that I string, or hurt one of my men or cattle, I'll ride on you and hang you from the stoutest limb I can find!"

Cardigan watched the color drain from the old man's face, and clamped his cold cigar between his teeth. He glanced at the scowling hulk of Moose Dugan and said softly: "You. You big-mouthed, bragging yellow-back, I licked you once in a fair fight, and I'll do it again. You've been makin' fight talk for a year now, but I never paid much attention to it. Well, to-night I'm carryin' a gun. I'm going down on the gallery where the stink ain't so strong and smoke a cigar. If you can whip your shaking hand into shape, come on down. I'll be waiting for you."

Pete Kerry's older boy grinned at the expression that slashed Dugan's face and turned with Cardigan as he moved toward the door. Straight and Turkey Jack waited until they filed past them, then Turkey followed, closing the door, his right hand still curled around the butt of his gun. He followed Cardigan down the steps, crossed the lobby, and paused on the wide gallery. Kerry and Straight made a tight group along the darkened wall with their boys. Cardigan glanced across the street at the heavy wagon still tied in front of Rutherford's store. The big homesteader and his wife sat on the seat, quietly watching the hotel, and Cardigan guessed that Harry Rutherford had told them about him. Their blonde daughter watched Cardigan, the impact of her stare crossing the narrow street, but he could read nothing in her face. The boy, obviously her brother, sat beside her, his face open with interest. Turkey Jack nudged him as heavy steps sounded from behind.

Cardigan slipped out of his coat, draped it carefully across the porch railing. Moose Dugan stopped in the lighted doorway, and Cardigan's easy voice sailed across to him.

23

"That's a fool stunt, standing with your back to the light. Are you tired of livin'?"

Dugan cursed in his deep voice, and stepped away until ten feet separated them. He said: "This ain't right, Cardigan. I don't want it like this."

Cardigan laughed. He took the cigar from his mouth, holding it in his right hand. "When I flip this," he said, "you'd better draw." He rolled the smoke between his fingers and spun it into the dust.

Dugan's hand dropped, blurred, and leveled, his left palm wiping the hammer twice as Cardigan pulled his long-barreled .44. Cardigan heard the blaring blast, and the eight-inch barrel cleared leather as lead tugged lightly at his shirt sleeve. The recoil shoved the gun against his palm, and Dugan went back against the porch rail, the fallen gun *clattering* noisily down the steps. Blood gushed from between his fingers as he clutched his right hip. His strength left him, and he rolled, thrashing and moaning, in the dust as people boiled out of the saloon, two doors down. Cardigan thrust his Smith & Wesson into the leather as Amos Ackerman stepped through the hotel door, Bitter Creek close behind him. They stared unbelievingly at the downed gunman.

Cardigan said evenly—"Tell the sheriff how it was, Amos."—and stepped down into the street, Turkey Jack walking a pace to the rear. The yelling and calling set up a dull clamor behind him, as he strode to the high wagon, stopping by the left front wheel.

The big man stared at him fixedly, and Cardigan caught the young woman's look of open interest. He swept off his high-crowned hat, exposing loose brown hair, and said: "You know who I am, and I can guess who you are."

"Are you telling us to get out of town?" the homesteader asked in a deep voice.

24

Cardigan glanced at the woman beside him. Her face was set in studied patience, as if she was accustomed to this.

"Yes," Cardigan said. "Take the Old Post road south for fifteen miles. Turn east on the wagon road for another ten. You'll come to a cañon there . . . we call it Devil's Gorge . . . go through it until you come to the valley beyond. There, you'll find a line shack, not much perhaps, but it will do until you get a place built."

An amazed expression crossed the man's face, and his wife tightened her grip on his arm. "Why, Cardigan?"

Cardigan glanced at their daughter, feeling the pull of her beauty, and moved his eyes away quickly. "Call it a whim, if you like."

"Let's not." The girl's voice was soft. Cardigan looked at her boldly then, and she added: "You baited that man, gave him two shots, and yet you didn't kill him. Why didn't you?"

Cardigan shrugged. "What good would it have done? Call that another whim, perhaps."

She shook her head, and the braids stirred. "I don't think you're the kind of man that would do anything on a whim . . . from crippling a man instead of killing him, or allowing a homesteader to move on your land." She took a deep breath, and asked: "What reason do you have for using us?"

"I use no one," Cardigan declared, and then asked: "What is your name?"

"Lila Overmile. This is my father, Jim . . . my mother, Amy . . . and my brother, Bob. Again I ask you, what do you want with us?"

"Nothing," Cardigan maintained. "Except good neighbors. What more? The land is good, and it's free. I run cattle on it and reserve the right to pick my neighbors. If you get hard up for meat, one of my riders will see that you get a side of beef to carry you through. But I never want to find out

25

you've mavericked one of my steers."

"What if a man steals one of your steers, Mister Cardigan?"

He looked at Lila, knowing she would not be frightened by his answer, and said evenly: "I'd hang him from the nearest tree."

She smiled then, and it puzzled him. He swung his head as Jim Overmile said: "That's fair, Cardigan, but we've had trouble before, and I can't help feeling there's a catch to this."

"There is," Cardigan agreed. "But it's a catch that won't be too unpleasant for either of us." He stepped back, and put his hat on. "I'll call on you within a month."

He waited until Overmile slapped the horses and saw Lila studying him as they drove slowly down Comanche Street.

He turned as Turkey Jack touched him. Four Leaning Seven riders were carrying Dugan away on a shutter. Cardigan lit a fresh cigar, listening to the sounds of the town die, and idly stroked his mustache.

Turkey Jack grunted, and said: "Every time you stroke them lip whiskers, I expect anything."

Cardigan watched the high, thin shape of Amos Ackerman as he stood with Bitter Creek by the hotel.

"Trouble there," Turkey Jack opined, and turned as Cardigan moved toward the livery stable.

Bob Harris stood in the darkened maw of the doorway, the red glow of his corncob pipe a winking eye in the darkness. He straightened as Cardigan and Turkey Jack approached, jerked a thumb toward the faint glow of a hanging lantern within. "Saddled and waitin', Wes." He pursed his lips and spat into the dust before adding: "Five years of layin' off ain't harmed your shootin' none." He swiveled his head to watch

Turkey Jack enter for the mounts. "Thought old man Ackerman was gonna be carried out." He shrugged his shoulders, and sighed heavily. "Guess a man can't have everything."

"Might not be war, after all," Cardigan prophesied. "Ackerman doesn't want to lose the men."

Harris shook his grizzled head, and knocked the dottle from his pipe. "Uhn-uh . . . not with Bitter Creek on the Leaning Seven. Ackerman cottons to the killer like he was a long lost son. He never would have put up a fight without that gunny proddin' him into it. After tonight, there ain't no doubt in Bitter Creek's mind what he's gonna do with you. He'll walk careful, and scheme close like he always does, but watch out. Bitter Creek will nail you if he gets a chance."

"What is there about him, Harris? Why does the old man put up with him?"

Studying his feet, Harris said—"Couldn't say."—and closed his mouth with a snap as Turkey Jack paused in the door.

Cardigan shot a glance between them, then swung up into the saddle.

"Remember what I told you, Wes," Harris reminded him.

Turkey Jack wheeled his horse and stopped, looking down on the man. "Why don't you shut your mouth? You talk too much."

Bob Harris moved away, muttering: "Maybe I do."

Cardigan backed the blue close to his foreman, and said— "Come on."—and moved off into the night. He lifted the horse into an easy trot a few miles from town, listening to the lulling drum of the hoofs. Before him, the land curved upward in gentle sweeps, toward the high country that was his empire. They rode in silence, and Cardigan saw her again in his mind's eye—the golden hair shining palely in the light from Rutherford's store. He remembered the gently swelled breasts and the soft curve of her hips outlined against the flowing folds of her simple, gingham dress. The thought of her filled him with a longing he had never known before, and now his empire seemed insignificant, his comfortable ranch home an empty place.

Turkey Jack broke into his thoughts: "You ought not to have treated Julia that way. The girl likes you."

Cardigan smiled at Turkey Jack's heavy-footed remark, and rode a way in silence before answering. "We know each other too well. There never was much between us . . . too one-sided."

"Is that a sin? There's a lot of men that would be happy to have her."

Cardigan turned his head and peered through the darkness at the older man. "Like her, don't you?"

"I'd give her my life, if she wanted it," Turkey Jack said simply.

Cardigan sobered, knowing how deeply the old man's feelings ran. Turkey Jack had put her on her first pony, had taken care of her bumps and bruises. It was all in the past for the old man, a part of Turkey's life that was strange and secret from Cardigan. Turkey Jack never talked of his life with Amos Ackerman, the life he had known before Ackerman moved north twelve years ago. Cardigan opened his mouth to speak of it now, but closed it, realizing it was none of his business. He shifted in the saddle, letting the miles melt beneath the blue's hoofs.

III

Cardigan shifted the tally book aside, and threw a leg over the arm of his chair. He extracted a cigar from the cubbyhole in his desk, wiped a match aflame on the rough leg of his chaps. He eyed Turkey Jack through the smoke. "All right, out with it. Something's been eating on you since breakfast."

The old man straightened, slapped the desk. "Dammit, I hate to tell you this!" He scrubbed his rough hands together, and added: "The boys want to quit!"

Cardigan smothered his amazement, by studying his long fingers, and asked quietly: "All of them?"

"Yep," Turkey Jack said. "Slats, Harry, Joe, Slab . . . even Ed-John."

"What's their complaint?" Cardigan asked.

"Nothin' you can put your finger on. Some of the boys have been takin' a ribbin' in town about being nurses now instead of hell-raisin' cowpunchers. There's also been a little talk about the fence. They dug the holes and strung the wire blockin' Leaning Seven from Sunrise, and they get kidded about their feet fittin' a spade better'n a stirrup."

Cardigan stood up and circled the room slowly. He paused by the window, looking out over the land that swept to the higher hills beyond. His herd of blooded bulls grazed contentedly under a brassy autumn sun. He swung back to face his foreman. "All right, Turkey, I never held a man against his will. Have the men drive the bulls to the north near the fence where they'll be safe until I hire some new men. They ought to be back late tonight, and I'll have their money waiting for them."

"Think it's smart to bed them critters down so close to the fence? We been waitin' a month now, and Amos ain't done nothin' *yet*." He rubbed his big hands together. "Julia was over yesterday when you was out. She said her father sent to El Paso for gunmen."

"Natural thing," Cardigan said. He paused and asked suddenly: "What's Bitter Creek to Ackerman?"

Turkey Jack's face was inscrutable as he answered: "Nothin'."

Cardigan studied him. "You worked for Amos before you came here. Bitter Creek was seventeen then, a few years older than myself. You got into some kind of a wrangle over him, and switched brands. What was the wrangle about?"

Turkey Jack clamped his lips together and sat in sullen silence. Cardigan pounded the desk with his fist, and shouted: "Damn it, man, I'm threatened by a range war, and you sit there and sulk! My enemy's daughter rides into my camp and tattles on her own flesh and blood, and you expect me to believe she keeps her mouth shut when she goes home?" He made a disgusted motion with his hand, and leaned close to the old man. "You like her, you've always liked her, and you hold it against me because I don't love her. All right, that's your privilege, but I want to know about that crazy killer, Bitter Creek. You hate him, and it's my guess you left the Leaning Seven because of him. Now, I'll ask you again, what's he to Ackerman?"

Turkey Jack let out a ragged breath. "He ain't nothin'. It's true that I left because of him. There was a big cattle war when Ackerman ran a spread down south. I lost some kin because Bitter Creek killed a man and liked the taste of blood. He killed other men. My kin got killed. Me and Amos had a squabble over it. The law was on his tail, and he pulled up to come here. He promised to get rid of Bitter Creek, but the kid showed up here anyway. That's when I left. If I'd stayed, I'd have gunned him down, and Julia didn't want me to."

Cardigan slapped the desk. "Why? What's the reason behind it?"

Turkey Jack's face grew sullen, and he stood up, moving toward the door. "I said all I'm gonna say . . . even if you fire me." He watched Cardigan and let out his breath slowly when the tall man turned away.

Cardigan waved a hand as he said: "Get those bulls on the move. I'm going over to the Overmiles'."

He snaked the gun belt from his desk and fastened the buckle on his left hip. Turkey Jack waited in the open doorway.

Cardigan said—"Saddle the blue for me."—and listened to his fading steps, wondering what went on in the old man's mind.

Cardigan rode for two hours, studying the land although he knew it like the back of his hand. Devil's Gorge was three miles to his left. He sat atop the world in a huge, flattened bowl of rich valleys and protecting crags. To his right, and over a squat run of hills, lay the Leaning Seven, a hundred and thirty thousand acres of land. He felt no envy, knowing that Ackerman's range was generally poorer and more arid than his own rich plateau. This was the bone of contention, this land, and Cardigan knew Ackerman had always looked at it with envious eyes. Although his own land was higher, the mountains cut the raw wind and piled the snow on the far slopes, sheltering the spread, turning it into an ideal winter graze, with abundant grass and clear water. It had served them well for years, a token of Fred Cardigan's generosity, but now the younger Cardigan had an investment to pro-tect—his blooded bulls. They had cost him two hundred and fifty dollars a head, and he wasn't going to permit them to roam and breed another man's stock.

Cardigan let the horse pause for a drink in the bubbling creek, and pushed on. He cut through a stretch of timber, emerging an hour later in a small valley. He saw the fresh marks of saw and axe, and was faintly surprised to see the erect walls of a three-room cabin. Cardigan spotted Jim

Overmile and his son, high above the line shack, and watched them walk off the slope toward the partly raised cabin. Cardigan halted by the hollowed-out log that served as a watering trough. He saw Lila Overmile pause in the shanty door to wipe a strand of golden hair from her face with the back of her hand.

Amy Overmile's voice made a gentle murmur, as Cardigan dismounted, and Jim and Bob joined him halfway to the door.

"Thought you'd changed your mind, Cardigan," Jim said.

Cardigan smiled faintly, and brushed his mustache. "I don't change much," he said.

They made a place for him at the rough table, and Lila poured his coffee cup full. He glanced around him, noticing the hanging blankets separating the pole bunks from the rest of the room. Cardigan turned to Amy Overmile. "Sorry this place was such a mess, but it's the best I had to offer."

She made chirping sounds with her lips. "Don't you worry about us. This is just fine." She turned to the crude sink.

Cardigan glanced at Jim and found the big man studying him. He had a square, honest face, and his hands were blunt and rough. Jim Overmile smiled, but studied the words carefully in his mind before speaking. "My daughter asked you, and I'll ask you . . . why all this?"

Cardigan toyed with his cup. "It's simple. I want to raise shorthorns, but they take a little babying . . . you know, hand feeding. Now, a Texas cowboy is a pretty proud man. He won't break ground with a plow, or pitch bundles, and I'm not crazy enough to ask him to."

"I still don't see where I come in."

"You raise hay, and I'll buy it from you," Cardigan said.

Lila's soft voice swung his head around, and he was surprised to find that he wanted an excuse to look at her. "How much do you pay for hay, Mister Cardigan?"

"Eight dollars a ton."

Jim Overmile slapped the table. "Why, dammit, that's only a little over half what it's worth on the open market!"

"True," said Cardigan. "But I only want half your crop. The rest you can sell for fourteen dollars a ton. You have a husky boy here and two damned fine horses. I'll let you fence three sections for yourself."

Jim Overmile sucked in his breath. "Three sections? Why that's fantastic . . . a dream a man can carry all of his life and never realize!"

Cardigan grinned. "It isn't as much as Kerry and Straight got. They have more boys, and I allow a section and a half per son. That seems fair to me."

"Fair? God, man, you lean over backward!" He looked at his wife and son, and saw Lila looking at Cardigan. He shook his head. "I don't know what to say, Cardigan. You leave me speechless."

"My name's Wes," Cardigan said. "It's like I said. I like good neighbors. There ain't much sense for a cattleman to fight a man as poor as he is. The way I see it, the shorthorn will change the whole cattle picture in Texas once they catch on. They take less graze, and they bring more money. That means I can afford to give up some of my land and still make more money than I did before. I hand-pick my neighbors, and some of them that tried to squat on my range got run off, *pronto*. In a few years, you'll be harvesting other crops, and our hay deal will be a secondary thing. You have a right to prosperity the same as I do."

Lila sat down across from him, and leaned her elbows on the table. When she crossed her arms, Cardigan saw the soft, yellow down curling close to the skin. "You really believe the things you say, don't you?"

"Sure, why not?"

"It's a wonderful dream, but what of your trouble with that other man, Ackerman? What if he fights you, and you lose?"

Cardigan waved a hand absently. "He'll fight all right, but we can't all win, can we?"

"No," she said softly, "but it would be a shame if *you* lost."

She flushed then, as he raised his eyes and stared at her. He glanced down at his hands self-consciously, and murmured: "I'd better be riding."

She stood up, and came around the table to stand before him, her hands behind her. "There is nothing so useless as an extra woman in the house. I'll walk you to the edge of the timber."

Her straightforward approach to his innermost desires startled him, throwing him off stride. "It's over a mile," he said, but she smiled and turned toward the door.

Cardigan paused and said to Jim: "If you see any riders on horses that aren't branded Sunrise, I'd appreciate your sending the boy to tell me."

"I'll do just that," Overmile said.

He stood in the doorway while Cardigan crossed to his horse.

They stopped at the edge of the timber. Cardigan's high-heeled boots pinched from the unaccustomed walking. Lila Overmile sank down on the squaw carpet and patted a place beside her. He sat, and stretched his long legs gratefully. The cabin was a ragged splotch in the distance; a light breeze shook the pines.

"Is she your girl?" Lila asked bluntly.

Cardigan stifled his surprise. "No . . . but we've known

each other for a long time."

"She's on the other side, isn't she?" Her voice was a sweet, low sound.

The sun made its swing toward the west, and the shadows among the trees began to lengthen.

"Yes, she's on the other side, but sometimes I wonder just whose side she really is on."

"That's strange, coming from you. I can't imagine your being undecided about anything." She lowered her eyes, and he noticed that the lashes were very long, a delicate veil against her lower lids. "I'm sorry for what I said that night in town. I had no right to spout off like that."

Cardigan lay back, his hands behind his head. "Everyone's entitled to an opinion."

"But not that kind of an opinion." She rolled over so she could look at him. "I was so sure you were arrogant and cruel . . . I learned differently that night."

"Arrogance is something we all have, to one degree or another. A man has to live with it and try not to let it show too often." He pulled his hat over his eyes.

She took it away gently, and sailed it a few feet away. "Don't hide your face from me, Wes. Don't ever hide anything from me."

Her voice was a low, strumming chord, and he sat up suddenly, gripping her by the shoulders. "You don't know me, Lila. You've only met me twice in your life." Somehow he wasn't surprised that the nearness of her, and the touch of her round shoulders beneath his hands inflamed him. He looked into her eyes and felt himself pulling her to him, unable to stop himself. She came against him willingly, and her lips burned his mouth with a searching passion that struck him like a blinding ray of light after years of blindness.

He felt the muscles of her back move as she wrapped her

arms around him, and her firm breasts pushed against the worn flannel of his shirt. He ran a trembling hand through the gold of her hair, then he pulled away. His voice was unsteady. "This is foolishness . . . insane."

"How long does it take, Wes? Deny that you felt this way the first time you saw me. I read it in your eyes. Look at me and tell yourself that you didn't believe I was attracted to you."

She searched his face, and he smiled.

"See, you did feel it. If we both feel this way, what sense is there in pretending that it doesn't exist?"

Cardigan glanced at the lengthening shadows and stood up, pulling her to her feet. She made no attempt to move away from him, but stood with the supple outline of her body pressed against him. "I'll tell my mother and father tonight."

"Your father will wonder what kind of man I am," Cardigan said.

She smiled, stood on her tiptoes to kiss him. "He already knows," she said, and started to walk away.

"Wait!" he said. "How do you know I'll come back?"

Small puckers formed in the corners of her mouth, and a devil pulsated in the depths of her eyes. "We have kissed," she said simply. "You'll come back."

"You're a positive little witch, Lila."

"Aren't you a positive man?" she countered, and turned to walk sedately away.

Cardigan watched her for a long while before mounting his horse to ride into the timber.

IV

Lights bobbed across the verandah as he rode into the yard, and the riders were gathered in a loose knot by the well curbing.

Turkey Jack ran from the bunkhouse, a lantern waving wildly in his hand. Cardigan swung from the horse, elbowed his way to the center. Someone had hung a lantern by the well frame, and he saw Ed-John lying on a doubled blanket, grinning in spite of the pain that laced him. Cardigan saw the dark spread of blood on the rider's ripped pants' legs and cursed. He knelt beside the man and asked: "What the hell happened here?" He looked around him, the lantern sending winking shadows across the drawn faces of the men.

Slab pawed the dirt with his toe, and blurted: "Me and Ed-John and Harry and Slats was drivin' them critters like you ordered, boss. We bedded 'em down for a nice quiet night when all hell broke loose. Bitter Creek and three Leaning Seven riders snipped their way through the fence and cut down on us with rifles. They got three bulls the first volley, and we scattered. The herd started to mill, and, since there was considerable shootin', me and Harry and Slats lit out for help."

Cardigan shifted his eyes between Slats and Harry, a young, heavy-set 'puncher, lounging in the shadows. "You left this boy to stay out there all alone?"

"It was all right, boss," Ed-John said. "I was on the far side of the herd when they hit, and everyone figured I was a goner. I would 'a' been iffen it hadn't been for them danged bulls actin' the way they did. Some son-of-a-gun put a bullet through the shoulder of my horse, and I took a header into the grass. I guess then's when I busted this pin. Bitter Creek and those hairpins with him must 'a' figured I'm down for good, 'cause they lit out after Harry, Slats, and Slab. Me, I figured to get gored or trampled when them critters got the prod. You know how a longhorn is when he sees a man afoot . . . he'll gore, but these crazy doggies just went on grazin' and steppin' light around me." He made a small motion toward

37

his bloody leg. "I managed to work my way to the edge of the herd, and Harry and Slats picked me up and brung me here."

The murmuring rose in volume as they talked it over among themselves. Cardigan quieted them and said: "All right, now you can see the difference between a shorthorn and a wild Texas steer. You brush-poppers may think it's a lot more courageous to rope and brand one of those wild hellions, but if Ed-John had fallen among them, we'd have maybe found strips of bloody cloth and lost one of the best riders that ever forked a horse. You men wanted to quit. All right, quit then. Quit now! Quit, and get out."

They glanced at each other in silence. Slats cleared his throat. "Guess I'll stay on," he said, and the others took up the chorus.

Cardigan waited until they had talked it out, and said: "Fine, but we have a little chore to do. You boys take Ed-John to the bunkhouse and have Cookie set that leg." He waited until they had staggered away with their burden, then turned to Turkey Jack. "Bitter Creek must have snipped the wire along that mile stretch that's passable from Leaning Seven. Take Harry and Joe up there and put it up again."

"Now . . . tonight?"

"Why not? There's a moon." Turkey Jack turned away, but Cardigan's voice halted him. "Another thing. Leave Harry and Joe there with rifles. You can stay if you want. When Bitter Creek shows up again . . . and it's my guess he will . . . bring him back here to me."

Turkey Jack nodded. Cardigan touched another rider, known as Pussy Foot. "Here," he said. "I'll give you a note. Ride up to the line shack above Devil's Gorge and give it to the people living there." The man nodded, and Cardigan added: "Better hitch up the buckboard. You might bring a woman back with you. Ed-John'll need help."

The man trotted toward the barn. Cardigan tore the back from an old envelope and wrote:

Lila,

One of my men broke a leg. We can spare no one to stay with him. Will you come?

Wes

Pussy Foot wheeled the buckboard up, paused to accept the note, then stormed out of the yard.

Turkey Jack ambled in from the darkness and asked: "Where the hell's he goin'?"

"Errand."

He grunted at the short answer, and asked: "You comin'? We're ready."

"Later maybe."

"What makes you think he'll come back?"

"He's proud," Cardigan said. "He'll come back."

"Then what?"

"I don't know. You know the man better than I do. You're the one who hates him. I don't," Cardigan said.

Turkey Jack pressed his lips together and murmured: "He's a tough one, Wes."

"I lost three blooded bulls tonight and a damned good man was put out of commission. Be as rough as you like." He turned then, walking toward the house with long, angry strides.

Cardigan woke her when he threw another log on the fireplace. She threw the robe back, and he caught a brief glimpse of a rounded calf and a slim ankle as she swung her feet to the floor. The first pale streaks of dawn filtered into the living room, turning the shadows gray. Cardigan grinned at her, and asked: "A bad night?"

"Bad for him." She nodded seriously toward the bunkhouse. "He suffered a great deal, but he never complained." She turned around, facing away from him. "Rub the kinks out of my back. That settee is hardly the last word in comfort." She sighed contentedly as he massaged her back. "Wes, who is he?"

He raised his eyebrows. "Ed-John? A kid, all Texan, tough, proud, fast with a gun, who'll ride anything with hair on it."

"He's a gentle boy," she murmured.

"Most strong men are," he said mildly.

She spun around, and laced her arms around his neck. Her breath was sweet and warm against his cheek. "You know who did it to Ed-John, don't you?"

He nodded.

"What are you going to do to the man?"

He moved away from her, troubled by his earlier decision. He had no wish to lie to her, so he said softly: "Send him home across a saddle maybe. Maybe I'll let him go. I don't know."

"How does it end, then? With either you or him dead, or both? A woman holding you in her arms and crying her heart out because her dreams are ended . . . is that the way it'll end?"

Her words beat against him, and he waved his hand futilely. "I don't know, Lila . . . maybe. Things sometimes take a funny turn."

He crossed to blow out the lamp, then stopped, listening to the pounding hoofs in the ranch yard. He made the door in one driving leap, snaking the gun from his holster as light, hurried steps crossed the porch.

The door flew open. He lowered the gun as Julia

Ackerman halted at the threshold. Her hot eyes flickered over Lila, and Cardigan knew that she had read the whole thing wrongly. Her voice was cold and dead as she spoke. "Ask me what I'm doing here, Wes . . . go ahead, ask me!"

"What *are* you doing here?"

"I came to bring you the news. I came to tell you that you could be proud of the fact that your murder was committed, and you've no blood on your hands. That hateful Turkey Jack! Bitter Creek is dead! Turkey Jack tied his horse to our corral an hour before dawn. He'd hanged him!"

Cardigan opened his mouth and then, controlling himself, said: "All right, we have one crazy gunman less. What of it?"

"What of it!" she echoed. Her voice rose to a scream. "What of your promise? You promised me he wouldn't be harmed, and you lied. You broke your word to me!"

Cardigan opened his mouth to deny her charge, then realized it would be impossible to convince her. Turkey Jack had taken the opportunity chance offered him, and now Cardigan had to back him. He pulled his face into a cold mask. "Your own father has done no less."

"But *he* did it! He didn't send one of his flunkies out to pull the rope while he made up to a nester tramp!"

Cardigan's hand traveled in a vicious sweep, and he slapped her heavily. Julia staggered back as Cardigan snarled: "Get out of here! No one asked you to come around here blabbing your mouth off. Now, get out and don't ever come back!"

Tears rolled freely down the girl's face, and she fingered the angry splotch where Cardigan's hand had struck her. She crossed to the door, and paused there. "I loved you, Wes. I thought I could make you love me, but you were cold, very cold. Now, you've killed the love I had for you. I want to see you dead. I want to see you dead, and I'll dance a jig on your coffin." She spoke softly, but her voice was filled with a hatred Cardigan could hardly credit. She shot Lila a contemptuous glance and said: "Take him. I'm through with him. Enjoy him while you can!"

Julia, her head high, wheeled through the door. Cardigan listened to her boots pound off the porch, then the sound of her horse's hoofs fading into the distance. He fished in his pocket, and lit a cigar with fingers that shook.

Lila stepped close to him, pressing herself against his broad back, her arms around him. "Don't blame yourself. It's done now."

Cardigan turned slowly and said quietly: "No. It's just begun. Turkey Jack is a marked man, but he doesn't know it yet." He moved away from her and, taking his hat, went outside to saddle up his horse.

He paused a mile from the Ackerman ranch house, a loose cluster of buildings against the flatness, and dropped his gun belt to the grass. He lifted the blue into a trot, and a half hour later slowed to a walk as he crossed the littered ranch yard. When he saw Ackerman sitting on the wide verandah, he stopped and crossed his hands on the saddle horn.

"Just keep 'em there!" Amos called.

"My intentions are peaceful. I came to talk peace, not war."

"It looked like you wanted peace last night."

"A regrettable mistake," Cardigan said. "I don't suppose you'd believe me if I said I neither ordered that, nor had anything to do with it."

"No, I wouldn't," Amos said coldly.

"He worked for you, too," Cardigan said. "It started here on your ranch, this thing between Turkey Jack and Bitter Creek." He watched the old man, trying to gauge the effect of his words. "I want it to end, Amos. I don't know what Bitter Creek was to you, but I mean it when I say I want to bring it to an end."

"You're a dead man, Cardigan," Amos said, "and your fence is as good as tore down, and your blooded bulls shot."

Cardigan lifted the reins, and the old man stood up quickly, throwing the rifle to his shoulder in one smooth motion. Cardigan felt the muscles bracketing his stomach jump as the bore centered between his eyes.

Ackerman's voice was a hoarse croak. "Ride out before I squeeze off! Ride out! And the next time I see you, you'll be dead!"

Cardigan's face was pale beneath his tan as he turned his horse, letting him walk out of the yard. He didn't look back until he paused to retrieve his dropped gun belt. Then he leaned against the shoulder of his horse and shook. He waited ten minutes before swinging into the saddle.

V

He recognized Miles Straight's mare and Pete Kerry's roan as he passed the corral. He tied his horse by the barn, walked easily toward the men gathered on his porch. Lila moved among them, serving coffee and rolls, and Cardigan saw Jim Overmile leaning against the far corner of the porch. Rifles lay loosely stacked on the bottom step, and coat pockets bulged with cartridges. Cardigan paused with one foot on the bottom step, and gave Lila a wan smile before saying to the men: "What is this, a council of war?"

Pete Kerry bit off a generous chew and shoved it to the corner of his mouth. "Ain't you in the middle of a war?"

Cardigan shook his head. "Not your war."

"Damned if that's so," Straight said. "You gave us the land. If you lose, then we lose, too, and, dammit, I like it here."

Cardigan glanced at Overmile. "I still say it isn't your war. Take Lila home with you when you go back. Things may get a little rough."

"She won't come, Wes," Overmile said.

Cardigan raised his head as Jim's wife came out of the house, and sank into his rocking chair. He appealed to her. "Can't you make Lila see why I want her away from here?"

Amy Overmile smiled. "She's headstrong, Wes. It's one of her failings."

Cardigan glanced at the girl, and she smiled at him before going into the house. He scrubbed a hand across the stubble covering his face. His eyes burned, and his nerves felt stretched like a rawhide rope. He nodded solemnly, and sat down on the step. "You're right. I do need help . . . bad." He found a short stick and drew a map in the dust. "This is the way the land lies. This valley is higher than the land around us. There's a break in the mountains . . . a low pass, and that's where Bitter Creek and his men came through. That's where they'll come through again, but they have to cut that wire to make it."

"What are you figuring?" Straight inquired.

"Ackerman has men and a hate, now," Cardigan stated. "There's no telling when he'll strike, but I have to be ready for him when he comes. I have to have warning. I'll station you men up on the bluffs above Mix Cañon, and you can see for miles around . . . even at night. Work in eight hour shifts, and, when you see any movement below on the Leaning Seven, ride like blazes and tell me."

"That sounds good," Kerry said. "When do we start?"

"Tonight," Cardigan said, and went into the house.

★ ★ ★ ★ ★

The soft *squeal* of the door and a soft hand woke him. He took it, and pressed his lips against her hot palm. Lila sat on the edge of his bed as Cardigan pawed at the sleep lingering in his eyes. He rubbed the soft down on her arm, and asked quietly: "What is it?"

She nodded toward the door. "Turkey Jack is waiting out in the hall. He wants to see you, says it's real important."

Cardigan sat up. "What time is it?"

"After eleven."

"Your folks still here?"

Lila nodded. "Dad's up on the bluff. Mother's asleep in the spare room."

"Why aren't you in bed?" he asked.

He lit the lamp, and turned her so that she faced the light. He saw the tired lines around her mouth and the dark shadows beneath her eyes. He watched her lips change, and folded her in his arms with a quick hunger. Her lips moved under his, and she moaned softly. When they parted, he said: "You should go home now."

Lila shook her head stubbornly. "I'll never leave this house, Wes, not unless you tell me you no longer love me, or don't want me."

He compressed his lips, not liking the thought. "Well, send him in."

The door closed behind her, then opened again.

Turkey Jack leaned against it, and said sourly: "Takin' orders from a woman I don't like. Askin' her can I see you, I like even less."

Cardigan swung to face him, his face heavy with temper. "There's things about you that I find damned little pleasure in." He took hold of himself and asked: "What the hell do you want?"

"Got a message a while ago," Turkey said. "From Julia."

"So?"

"So, I'm goin' to her. She asked for me."

"Don't be a fool!" Cardigan said heatedly. "You can't trust her now!"

Turkey Jack shoved his gaunt old frame away from the door, his whiskers bristling. "You said enough! I don't have to take that kinda talk from no man . . . not about her!"

"Get some sense," Cardigan cautioned. "You've been a fool about Julia ever since I've known you."

"And before I knowed you," Turkey supplied. "I work for this brand, but that don't give you the right to tell me my business or how to pick my friends."

"Wait just a minute," Cardigan said. "You hanged a man without my say-so after I told you to bring him in. I let that go because I can see where a man's hate is sometimes something he can't help. I'm telling you now, Turkey . . . don't leave this ranch."

"I'm goin'," Turkey Jack insisted. "She asked for me, and I'm goin'."

Cardigan moved a step toward his holstered gun hanging from the back of a chair.

Turkey pulled his .44 with practiced speed. "Hold it, Wes. I had a hunch you'd be stubborn." He backed toward the door. "See you around, cowboy," he said, and closed the door behind him.

Cardigan listened to the fading drum of hoofs, and a moment later the soft steps of Lila as she came to his door. She entered as he sat on the edge of his bed, his head down, and she went to sit beside him. He looked at her, his eyes bleak. "He's a dead man, Lila, a dead man. I couldn't do a thing about it."

She gathered him to her, pillowing his head against her

breasts. "He had a right to choose. Grant him that right."

He raised his head suddenly and exclaimed: "Now, I can understand it!"

She watched him closely. "Understand what?"

"About Julia . . . why she was in a rage after Bitter Creek was killed." He stood up and paced the room. "They were always together . . . in town, even out here on the old man's ranch. There was always something between them, something sly, like they had a joke that no one else knew." His voice was incredulous. "She must have been in love with him."

She sat there, facing him, and her voice was calm. "I'd guessed that, too. There isn't much one woman can hide from another. I also had guessed that she loved you."

"I don't believe it," Cardigan snorted. "You can't be in love with two women, or two men at the same time . . . it just ain't natural." He shook his head, not understanding it, and moved toward the door.

"Where are you going?"

He stopped. "To sit on my front porch and wait for Turkey Jack to come back, tied across his saddle." He saw the hurt mount in her eyes, and added softly: "Get some sleep, Lila. I'll call you if anything happens."

He moved to the kitchen, pumping a tin cup full of water, and cut a wedge of stale pie. He ate half of it before his appetite left him. He glanced at the mirror, then spent a half hour shaving and carefully trimming his full mustache. He wandered into the yard, and back to the house. The hall clock struck two, and he crossed the carpeted room to wind it. When a dog barked out by the barn, he shuffled across the room to peer through the darkness at the disturbance. He broke out his cleaning gear and dismantled his .44, spending an impatient hour on the task. The clock chimed, and he rubbed his eyes as he crossed to sit on the porch.

He realized he had been dozing when his chin bumped his chest. He pulled himself awake with a start. He heard the horse snort by the watering trough and identified the dark shape before he left the porch. He crossed the dusty yard at a dead run and yelled when he touched the body lashed across the saddle. Men poured from the bunkhouse, half-clad figures with wildly waving lanterns.

Cardigan heard a door slam inside the house and knew he had awakened Lila with his yell. Harry and Joe cut the ropes holding Turkey Jack, and slid him to a blanket spread on the ground. Cardigan gave the pony a sharp slap on the rump, and the horse trotted toward the barn. Someone held up a lantern. Lila pushed her way between Slab and Joe to look at the dead man. She shivered and pulled her woolly robe tighter, leaning against Cardigan. He looked at her, and the lantern light made her face appear unnaturally pale, with deep shadows against her cheeks, in the soft V between her breasts. Cardigan motioned her away. She crossed to wait on the porch, her bare feet padding in the dust.

Slab cleared his throat and said to no one in particular: "They shot him through and through. He never got off a round." He handed Turkey's .44 to Cardigan, and he sniffed the barrel.

They were watching Cardigan, waiting for him to make the first move, but he only said—"Bury him."—and walked toward the house.

Lila on the porch pulled the robe tighter around her legs. "Well, it happened like you said."

Cardigan touched a match to his cigar. "Small comfort in being right," he said, then lapsed into silence.

"Why do you want to be the conscience of the world?" she asked softly.

Cardigan took the cigar from his mouth, surprised. "I didn't know I was."

"Aren't you? You let the homesteaders have land because you feel guilty about the way other cattlemen have treated them. You want to breed shorthorns because you feel you owe something to the destiny of Texas. You defied Ackerman, and yet you shouldered the responsibility of Bitter Creek's death without a murmur. Now, it's Turkey Jack. You're blaming yourself for that, too. What else can you call it, Wes?"

"Get some sleep," he said.

She nodded, knowing him well, realizing that there was nothing she could say to ease him. He was that kind of man, and she accepted it. He made his mistakes as he lived, unafraid, without apology to anyone, even himself.

Cardigan waited until he heard the door of her room close, then crossed to the barn. He spread the blanket carefully and drew the cinch. He mounted, letting the horse buck until the ginger left him, and swung out across the land.

He had no plan in mind, only the driving desire to put an end to death. He thought of Turkey Jack and smiled wryly, realizing the girl was right—he was blaming himself. He could see the places clearly, the times when he should have given way to Ackerman and avoided this fight. He felt no fear, only a deep sense of responsibility toward the innocent people who were now embroiled in his troubles.

Finally he cut out of the timber to pause overlooking the Ackerman ranch buildings. He thought of Lila, wondering if she would be awake now. He passed the corner of the barn as Julia Ackerman emerged from the front door, stopped for a heartbeat to stare at him, and then yelled for her father.

Wes Cardigan watched her, seeing the pale fright stamped on her face, and the rigid pose of her curved body. The screen door slammed, and Amos Ackerman stood with his back against it, his rifle held loosely in his hands. Cardigan halted as the old man raised the Winchester and said to him: "I've had enough, Amos. Let's settle it between us now."

Old Amos snarled, and worked the lever as Julia stood there in wide-eyed fascination.

Cardigan felt his heart hammer wildly, but made no move toward his holstered gun. "I want peace, Amos," he said. "Even if I have to die for it."

"You will at that!" Amos yelled. He drew a bead. Then Cardigan saw Julia struggling with her father, heard the muffled explosion followed by her sharp scream. She staggered to the edge of the steps and went off in a sprawling tumble.

Amos cried out, and stumbled from the porch, fired rifle forgotten, and gathered the girl in his arms. He folded her tenderly against him and rocked her back and forth, tears coursing down the creases of his face.

Wes knelt beside Ackerman, straightened the girl's dress. Julia rolled her head weakly. "I'm so sorry, Wes. I never stopped loving you."

Cardigan felt the tears sting his eyes. "No, no, don't talk. We'll get a doctor."

She shook her head faintly. "It's all right, Wes. You were right the first time you came here. It would have been better to have left Bitter Creek unavenged. There has been enough killing." She turned to her father, pain causing her slim body to arch. She coughed, and Cardigan wiped the bloody foam from her lips with his handkerchief.

The Leaning Seven hands made a tight circle around them. Amos murmured, dazed: "What have I done . . . what have I done?"

"Don't cry, Papa, it's better this way. It's . . . it's ended now." Her eyes moved to Cardigan, and she whispered: "Would it help you to understand if I told you Bitter Creek was my brother?"

He opened his mouth to speak, but she slumped back, and died in the old man's arms.

Amos raised his eyes to Cardigan at last. "He was no good. I knew that, but I loved him . . . and she loved him, enough to betray an old friend to avenge him. He cost me my life's work once, and I forgave him. Now, he's cost me my daughter." His chin sank down on his chest, and he was silent. Cardigan touched him, and the old man stirred beneath his hand. "Go home, Cardigan, and let's try to live like men again."

Cardigan wanted to speak, to say something that would ease the old man's grief, but he knew there were no words. He stood up, turned quickly, then mounted his horse.

He rode from the yard, not looking back because he knew there was nothing for him to see that he wouldn't see a thousand times before he died. There was his land ahead of him, stretching as far as his eyes could see. He saw his cattle grazing on a far slope, and he knew that it had not changed—only he had changed.

He thought of Lila, waiting at his house. The thought bolstered him in this hour of revelation. He touched the blue with his heels, and lifted him excitedly into a hurried lope.

THE BIG KILL

I

Somewhere along the trail of John Saber's thirty-two years, the lure of easy money had endowed him with sufficient perception to understand a thief. The man who lied was no longer a mystery to Saber for he could recall times in his life when he had felt a deep reluctance to face the truth about himself. This wisdom affected John Saber until he held himself aloof from other men, walking among them, but somehow feeling that he walked above them.

He waited while the train passed him, to disappear down the twin ribbons of steel, leaving only the memory of noise, the smell of hot oil, and the unsteadiness in his long legs produced by three days on the swaying coach. He carried no luggage, which caused the station agent to give him a cursory inspection. He had blond hair, nearly white at the temples, and blue eyes set deeply above an aquiline nose. A tawny mustache hid his mouth, and a thin cigar jutted from between his clenched teeth. Loungers by the Texas Pacific Express Office gave him a careful scrutiny. The flat hat sat evenly on his head, and a black coat covered an immaculate white shirt. The gun their eyes probed for lay under his left armpit in an upside-down holster.

John Saber raised a finger in a perfunctory gesture, and said: "Direct me to Wes Cardigan's ranch."

The urge to refuse was plain on the face of the man he addressed, but some light in Saber's level eyes held his tongue. "First road south of town . . . follow it for fifteen miles. You can't miss it."

Saber nodded his thanks, an almost imperceptible movement of his head, and turned toward the livery, two blocks away.

The man watched him until he disappeared around the end of the building, then turned to another lounger.

"Think it's him?"

"Maybe. Wes said he'd bring in a man if things got worse. Didn't see no gun, though."

"Go get a horse and tell Bodry," the man said, and settled down again as his friend scurried toward Comanche Street.

John Saber studied Hondo's main street as he paced its length. The Alamo House sat on the corner, and across from it Rutherford's store. Keno Charlie's saloon made a wide-fronted splash in the middle of the block, and small, slab-sided buildings filled out the town.

Bob Harris's Livery Stable set at the end of the street. Saber paused in the archway, the Texas sun beating down, intense and hot. Harris straightened in his chair, laying the magazine aside.

"A horse," Saber said.

Harris retreated into the stable, the sound of thrashing coming mildly amid his good-natured cursing. He emerged a few minutes later leading a close-coupled bay.

Saber walked around the horse, examining it thoroughly, and said at last: "A little rabbit-breasted, isn't he?"

Harris's eyes showed shock. "The idea!"

Saber placed a foot carefully in the stirrup, and mounted.

53

He paused, looking down at Harris, saying: "Put this on Wes Cardigan's bill."

"Friend of his?" Harris pried.

"Regardless, he will pay for the use of the animal."

Saber smiled faintly at the frustration that flitted across Harris's face, and swung the horse south, lifting him into a trot as the last building of Hondo faded behind him.

He rode for an hour, studying the land as it climbed ever higher. Behind him now lay the flatness of the desert, and the color of the soil beneath the horse's hoofs changed from a red loam to a rich black-brown. As he moved higher, small trees appeared in isolated patches, thickening as the road wound upward. He paused, two hours from town, on a high bench overlooking the country below, and dismounted to ease the horse and build himself a smoke.

There was that studied patience in Saber that came out in the little things he did. His fingers worked on the paper holding the loose tobacco. Gently, slowly, the cylinder formed, ready at last for the flick of his tongue that would complete it. Saber rolled it between his blunt fingers, and, satisfied at the evenness of the pack, the parallel lines he had formed, he laid it between his lips and applied a match.

He drew long on the cigarette, content with his thoughts, coming alert only when he heard the distant rattle of a hard-driven buckboard. He watched the rig careen around a bend in the road, and his face changed, his lips thinning, his pale eyes growing sharp. He saw that a man was driving, and a woman clung to the pitching seat with one hand, the other clutching a bonnet that threatened to fly off.

John Saber made a trim, high shape there in the road, his fawn trousers tucked neatly in polished half boots, and the man sawed the blowing horses to a halt. Dust billowed up, and a faint irritation crossed Saber's face.

The man mopped the sweat from his face and asked bluntly: "Lost?" He was nearing fifty, graying at the temples, with a face that was criss-crossed with well-used wrinkles.

"No," Saber said. "Just resting the horse."

Saber glanced at the woman and saw that she was regarding him levelly, a faint flush in her cheeks. She was young, with a ripely molded body, and lovely dark eyes.

"I'm Buck Bodry," the man said. "This is my woman, Edith. I've made that ride from Hondo to the rim in an hour and a half flat many times." The man's voice was loud, and a strong current flowed below the surface of it. The woman turned her head and silently regarded her folded hands.

"You must have a great many horses," Saber said.

"I do things sudden," Bodry said. "Horses, a fight, or a woman. I like 'em fast." He laughed loudly at his own humor, and slapped the woman resoundingly on a rounded thigh. She glanced at Saber, blood mounting her face, then moved to the far edge of the seat, staring fixedly at the floorboards.

Bodry grunted, lifted the reins, then lashed the team into a plunging run. Saber watched. The woman turned in the seat, giving him a long look. He read the appeal in her eyes—it was that plain—and raised his hat before she turned back to stare over the horses' rumps.

He waited until the dust spiral dwindled before the breeze, then placed his foot carefully in the stirrup and mounted. He rode on slowly, thinking of the woman who was Buck Bodry's wife. He remembered her as clearly as though she were before him still—that faint apology in her eyes, the haunting sadness around the corners of her mouth. Saber let her occupy his thoughts until he came to the fork in the road and the fence that announced his entrance to Sunrise graze.

He gave the cattle a careful scrutiny. The land, rich and

lush, lay in the high valleys and watersheds formed by a gla-
cier cut a million years before man. It was the land of the
shorthorn Hereford. They lolled, grazed, dotting the land
with their uniform red hides, white faces, and white-lined
backs. Saber lifted the reins, urging the bay into a trot, and
held that pace until he saw the scattered ranch buildings a
mile ahead.

Wes Cardigan was on the porch and stood up as Saber
rounded the corner of the bunkhouse to dismount by the
watering trough. A cowpuncher came from the barn at a lope
and led the bay away. Cardigan stepped down, a tall man with
lead-gray eyes and a full, reddish-brown mustache. He shook
Saber's hand warmly.

"A long time, Wes," Saber said. "A damned long time."
He smiled then, wrinkles forming at the corners of his eyes,
but the gravity never quite leaving his face.

"I expected you last week," Cardigan said. "Come on into
the house."

Saber followed him onto the porch and said evenly: "A
man travels slow but gets where he's going."

Cardigan halted then, and turned. He regarded Saber for a
moment. "Maybe, John . . . maybe. But this is turning into a
sudden country."

"You're a sudden man, Wes. You don't really need me to
handle your troubles."

"Maybe," Cardigan said again, and opened the screen
door.

Saber stepped into the cool of the room, sweeping off his
hat as Cardigan's wife turned from the dining room table to
face him.

"Lila," Cardigan said, "this is John Saber. John, my wife,
Lila."

"A pleasure, ma'am," Saber said.

She was, he thought, the loveliest woman he had ever seen. Her hair was a pale gold, her eyes a shade of gray that was almost green. She smiled as she turned away, and John Saber's eyes glowed with admiration.

Wes Cardigan chuckled. "She is beautiful, isn't she?"

Saber agreed. Cardigan went ahead into the big ranch kitchen, toeing a chair aside for Saber. Lila crossed to the stove and poured the coffee cups full, then pulled a chair back for herself. She sat across from them, arms crossed, regarding Saber with a frank appraisal that made him uneasy. He had the feeling that she could see right through him and lifted his coffee cup quickly to hide his discomfort.

"I was surprised to get your letter, Wes. I had no idea you were having trouble."

Cardigan traced a design on the oilcloth with his fingertip. "I had my share of trouble five years ago. I thought it was over, but I was wrong. This is something I've got to have outside help on. I can't take the law into my own hands and do it alone."

"I met Buck Bodry and his wife on the way here. There's something off there. . . ." His voice caused Lila to swing her eyes back to him.

"Does Bodry know who you are?" Cardigan asked.

"No. No one knows who I am." Saber set the cup down.

"Wes, I'm a federal officer. I have to have more to go on than what you told me in your letter." He waved a hand. "I talked it over with the captain and took a month's leave, but he'll only sanction my acts here officially if I uncover something solid to go on."

Cardigan pounded the table with his fist. "John, I'm being rustled blind! So is every cattleman in the area."

"You've a sheriff, haven't you?"

"*Agh,*" Cardigan said and reached for his coffee cup.

"It won't do any good to get angry, Wes," Lila said softly.

Cardigan scrubbed a big hand across his face, and blew out a long breath. He lit a cigar, then said: "When old man Ackerman died, he made arrangements for Buck Bodry to take over his spread . . . a hundred and thirty thousand acres."

Saber whistled. "That's a great deal of land for one man to control. I'm surprised the homesteaders haven't cut it up. After all, this is Eighteen Hundred and Eighty-Two and Texas is facing the end of an era."

"They won't cut up the Leaning Seven," Cardigan said grimly. "Bodry has his land patrolled now. A man isn't even allowed to cross it. Every time one of my riders crosses the fence, he gets a bullet thrown his way."

"Has he been hit bad by the rustlers?"

"Damned if I know," Cardigan said. "He says he has, but who can tell? I want you to take a ride through his place, take a look around. There's plenty of holes up in those badlands where a whole herd could be hid out."

Saber fashioned a cigarette with great care. He lit it. "You want me to get shot?"

"Knowing you," Cardigan said, "I don't think you would."

"No man is immune to a bullet," Saber said.

Lila said: "Tell him what Ed-John and Slats said, honey."

"It's a funny thing, John," Wes said, "but two of my 'punchers claim some of my rustled cattle have come back."

"How's that?" Saber asked, surprised.

Cardigan leaned forward and idly stroked his mustache. "The way I've got it figured is that they've been rustlin' my herd just about the time they're ready to calf. They hold the cow until the calf is dropped, then keep the calf, and slip the cow back to me. That way there isn't anything around with my brand on it. It would take a big place to hide a herd of stolen calves. A man would also have to have a guard over his property because nothing is more suspicious than a growing calf crop . . . especially when they're bein' dropped two and three times a year."

"And you think Buck Bodry's hiding those cattle?"

"What else?" Cardigan said. "I thought for a while they'd been driven up into Arizona, but my riders swear they're bein' pushed back into the herd . . . minus the calves. Slats recognized one where he'd made a slit with his knife and cut the vent too long. Ed-John says he's seen three he knows particularly. When I got it figured out, I wrote you."

Saber gave it considerable thought, then said: "That's a new trick. I'll need a couple of good men who know the land and can shoot straight, if we have to."

"Willie and Burt Kerry," Cardigan said without hesitation. "Willie's the oldest, about twenty. The two of them know every foot of Bodry's place. They ran wild over there after my trouble with Ackerman was over."

"Fine," Saber said, and stood up. "I'll get an early start in the morning."

Cardigan shook hands with him, and Lila touched Saber on the arm. "I'll show you to your room." She turned, and he followed her down the hall.

He laid his hat squarely on the dresser top, tested the bedsprings with an outstretched hand. Lila stood in the doorway, the dying sun streaming through the hall window to outline her in her gingham dress. Saber pulled his eyes away from her quickly, thinking again of Edith Bodry and the gentle turn of her body as she sat beside her husband on the buckboard.

"Edith is a beautiful woman, isn't she?"

Saber's head came up quickly. He controlled his surprise

with an effort. His first impulse was to deny that Edith Bodry filled his thoughts, but he changed his mind and admitted: "Yes, there's something about her. I noticed it right away."

"The girl made a bad bargain," Lila said evenly. "Don't blame her for it."

"How can I blame anyone? I don't know her."

"What is there to know about a woman?" Lila asked. "The first night I met my husband I knew that I would love him . . . it was that strong between us. I am not the only woman in the world who thinks like that."

"That's nonsense," Saber declared. "There is no place in my life for a woman."

Lila smiled gently—"Then I feel sorry for you, John."—and closed the door.

Saber stared at the blank panel, puzzled by her words, and a little worried. His life was simple because he kept it that way. He sat down on the edge of the bed, pulling at his boots. Lila's voice carried through the house, and Saber paused as he heard her laugh.

It's been a long time since I heard a woman's laugh, Saber thought. He stretched out on the bed, falling asleep immediately.

II

Bacon sizzled and the rich aroma of strong coffee carried through the house. Saber paused in the archway of the kitchen as Cardigan and the two young men at the table raised their heads.

"John, this is Willie and Burt Kerry. Boys . . . John Saber."

Willie was all bones and length, towering over his younger brother by four inches. His quick smile, brief handshake, and the worn .44 riding his hip told Saber that he was all business.

Burt gave Saber's hand the fleeting pressure of a man who considers handshaking a waste of time, and said: "Just in time for Lila's pancakes."

Saber slid back his chair, and ate his breakfast with a relish. Lila said nothing, nor did she give any indication of her thoughts, but Saber caught her watching him at least once when he raised his head.

"I've explained the deal to Willie and Burt," Cardigan said. "You can make any further plans you want when you get there."

"Where can we establish a camp and still remain undetected?" Saber wanted to know.

"The best place would be on this side of the fence, near Bodry's boundary line. There's some damn' rough country up there, and a man can see for miles around him." Willie shoved back his chair. "We're ready, any time you are."

"All right," Saber said, and stood up. He turned to Wes Cardigan. "If there's any word, I'll send one of the boys back. It might be that I'm going to need help."

Cardigan nodded.

Saber gave Lila a smile, then placed his hat squarely on his head, and followed the Kerry boys to the barn.

Burt had saddled the livery bay, and Saber swung up, following them out of the yard.

They rode in silence for over a mile, then Willie asked: "You carryin' a gun?"

Saber smiled and nodded, dropping his eyes briefly to Willie's revolver. "What is yours?" he wanted to know.

"Merwin and Hulbert, Forty-Four. Wanna look at it?" He didn't wait for an answer but flipped it up and out, extending it butt first to Saber.

Saber hefted it expertly, then reached under his coat,

handing over a cedar-handled Frontier. Willie turned it in his hands, saying: "It's safe to shoot a little. Wanna try it out?" He nodded to the gun in Saber's hand.

Burt watched this with a deep interest, leaning forward intently to study Saber's face.

"Pick it out," Saber said, and turned his head to follow Willie's pointing finger. He saw the remains of an old campfire thirty yards away, the blackened coffee can placed alone on a flat rock. He nodded, and Willie cocked the Frontier, sending his bullet slightly below and a little to the right of the can.

Saber's hand moved, and Willie's .44 blasted the morning air, the tin can tumbling off the rock. Willie shot again. The can sailed up, disappearing in the grass. Willie's grin was immense, a pleased slash across his face as he handed the gun to Saber. He slid his .44 back in his holster and said—"I guess you'll do."—and lifted his horse into a trot.

They paused an hour later, and Willie Kerry pointed to a long slope dotted with bunch pine. "We can hole up in there. Plenty of rocks to hide us and wood for a fire."

"I'm satisfied," Saber said. "Settle down some place up there, and I'll take a ride over to Bodry's and have a talk with him."

"All right," Willie said, "but be careful. There's three men on Bodry's payroll that'll shoot first and question the corpse later . . . Bill Dent, Ernie Stiles, and Jules Lurch."

Burt said: "You'll know Dent because he's stocky and wears a pearl-handled gun, backwards. Stiles is taller than you, with brick-red hair. He don't wear a gun where you can see it. Lurch is new. I never seen him."

Saber listened to this with a smooth face, then nodded. "Expect me back by nightfall."

"And if you ain't?" Burt asked pointedly.

"Let's worry about that when the sun goes down," Saber said, and moved away at a lope.

He crossed the fence line a few minutes later, riding in a southeasterly direction. The land fell away from him in a shallow run, and he noticed the change in the grass. On the side of the hills, the sun had baked it a pale brown, almost yellow, and so it went for miles, uninterrupted by the seeps and springs that dotted Cardigan's range. Saber glanced behind him, seeing the buttresses at his back looming. He studied the land around him thoroughly, letting a natural instinct within him catalogue each rise, each depression, until he understood it as well as the men who habitually rode it.

On his left a grove of stunted pines rose to break the monotony, and Saber gave their edge a sharp attention. When he saw the horseman at the fringe, watching him, he swung the bay's head, moving toward the rider at a brisk trot.

He recognized Edith Bodry with a start when he was a hundred yards away, but continued his gait, pulling up before her a few minutes later. He swept off his black hat.

Edith Bodry watched him with worry in her dark eyes and said: "It's not safe for a man to ride on this land."

"Do you wish me off, ma'am?" Saber's voice was pleasant, and an interest rose momentarily in her eyes—then was gone.

"My husband would be displeased should he find you here."

"From our brief encounter yesterday, I should judge that he finds little that does not displease him," Saber said.

"You've come from the Cardigan Ranch," Edith stated. "You couldn't be my husband's friend then."

"Has your husband many friends?"

"No," Edith said honestly, "he doesn't believe in them."

Saber looked at her boldly, and she did not flush beneath his gaze. He divined then that she welcomed his attention, and he dismounted, inviting her to do likewise by lifting his hand. She was a small weight beneath his hands as he lifted her down. The swell of her bosom, pulled tightly against her shirt-waist, caused him a moment's confusion before she stepped away.

"This is . . . all wrong," Edith said, but sat down. Saber lowered himself beside her, and plucked idly at the grass. "I think Buckley hates you," she added.

Saber showed no surprise. "How could he? He doesn't know me!"

"Does one bull know another when he lowers his head and charges blindly? Whatever it is, he hated you before the first spoken word."

"I hate no man," Saber stated.

"Perhaps not," Edith said, "but it won't stop him. You weren't impressed by him yesterday. It infuriated Buckley." She took a long breath. "For the first time in over a year, I was happy . . . for a moment."

She stopped, cocking her head to one side as if listening. Saber opened his mouth to speak, but she held up her hand, pointing to a rider some distance away.

"Ernie Stiles," she said. "Buckley has sent him after me."

Saber stood up, pulling her to her feet, her hand resting lightly on his arm. She watched Stiles, and Saber watched her, noticing how long her eyelashes were, and the way her full mouth pulled into a bow.

He said: "Since we are both riding in the same direction, I suggest we ride together."

Her face mirrored a fleeting panic, and she said quickly: "Oh, no. That will only mean trouble."

Saber smiled, and lifted her to her horse. "Both of us, I think, may claim trouble as an old friend." He swung up on the bay.

Ten minutes later they met Stiles. The man's red hair showed beneath the pushed back brim of his hat. It was a wild, disarrayed shock of hair, and Saber sensed that the other was proud of it.

Stiles kept his eyes on Saber and said curtly, disrespectfully to Edith: "Get back to the ranch house. Buck wants you."

Saber's eyes bored into Stiles's, and he said coldly: "If you are addressing the lady, her name is Missus Bodry. Now, repeat the message properly."

"What?" Stiles was genuinely surprised.

Saber crowded his horse near Stiles and whipped a hand up and across his face. A cold fury mounted in Stiles's eyes, but some warning in Saber's expression held him motionless. It had happened so suddenly, without warning, that he was uncertain. Saber took full advantage of that uncertainty. He lifted the reins, walking the bay around Stiles's horse, all the time cursing him, daring him to reach for the gun in his hidden holster. Stiles remained stiffened, hands half lifted, but made no further move.

Saber paused again in front of him. He snaked a large watch from his coat pocket and held it in the palm of his left hand. "I'll give you exactly fifteen seconds to dismount with your hat in your hand, and apologize. If you don't, you're a dead man."

Edith Bodry watched, wide-eyed, as Stiles dismounted carefully, hat held in hands that were not quite steady. He mumbled something, and Saber nudged the bay closer, kicking the man solidly in the ribs. Stiles staggered, but caught himself.

He shot Saber a loaded glance and said again, more clearly: "I'm sorry, Missus Bodry, but your husband's wantin' you at the ranch house."

"Now, get on your horse and get out of here," Saber ordered.

Stiles mounted, and said with a soft wickedness: "This is something I won't forget, friend."

"You're not supposed to," Saber told him, and made a motion of dismissal.

Stiles wheeled the horse and rode away, not looking back.

Saber studied the retreating back for a long moment, then turned to Edith Bodry. "Shall we go now?"

She nodded, but made no move. Her eyes glowed with an emotion Saber couldn't place, as she said huskily: "I knew you were dangerous the first time I saw you, but I had no idea how dangerous until now. Stiles is a killer, and yet he was frightened. Somehow, I'm frightened, too."

"My only wish," Saber said, "was to please a lady." He watched the color climb into her cheeks, but did not smile after she turned her mount.

Buck Bodry rested on his wide front porch, never taking his eyes from his wife and the somber man riding beside her. Stiles stood at Bodry's right, anger still staining his cheeks, as Saber dismounted by the watering trough, lifting Edith Bodry from the saddle. He spoke a few soft words to her, then removed his hat, standing with it before him. Bodry made no move as they turned toward the porch, speaking only when Edith mounted the steps.

"I thought I told you not to ride today!"

"It slipped my mind," Edith said quietly.

"I'll bet it did," Bodry said. "I'll bet it slipped your mind that you're my wife, too!"

Edith gasped, and Saber placed his foot carefully on the bottom step, folding his hands on his knee. "If you're inferring that Missus Bodry and I met by prearrangement, I'll be glad to ram the words down your throat."

Buck Bodry gave Saber close attention. "Stiles said you was salty, but I discounted it then. You know, there could be a rifle or two at your back."

"In all probability there is, but I can draw and kill you before their bullets cut me down."

Bodry slapped the arm of his chair. "By God, you got gall! There ain't no rifles on you, friend. I just wanted to know what the hell you think you're doing on my ranch."

"I'm afraid I'm lost, after all," Saber said. "I met Missus Bodry by accident, and she was kind enough to ask me to dinner." He flicked his eyes to Edith and saw her quick smile.

"My wife's a fool," Bodry said, "and you must think I'm one, too. There ain't no invites passed out around here unless I make 'em, and you ain't on the callin' list. I got you figured now, Saber. I knowed you was workin' for Cardigan two hours after you stepped off that train." He stood up, his hand hanging conveniently near his gun. "Now, you turn that horse around and tell Cardigan that if he or any of his men set foot on my place, they'll get lead poisonin'."

"That," Saber said, "is as plain an offer as I've had today."

He straightened, and moved toward his horse. Edith Bodry remained on the porch, watching him. Saber turned his head, gazing at the grove of stunted pines two miles away, and then whipped his eyes back to her. The meaning in the look was as clear as a spoken word. He felt his heart quicken as she smiled fleetingly, then turned away into the house.

Stiles watched Saber with a flat-faced hatred. Saber grinned at him, then wheeled his horse, and galloped from the yard.

He held that pace until he came to the grove of trees, then paused to rest the horse. He pulled his hat lower over his eyes, and studied the land. The sun was making a vertical stand in the heavens and the Bodry ranch buildings were a dark spot in the distance. He became alert when a small bush rustled. He saw a large rabbit pause twenty feet away, pale-bellied and pulsating.

Saber's hand went into his coat, and the short-barreled Colt shattered the serenity of the morning. The rabbit flopped once, then lay still. Saber returned the gun to the up-side-down holster, then crossed to pick up the rabbit. Satis-faction made him smile as he remounted.

It was a clear head shot.

Willie turned the rabbit over a low bed of coals. Burt sat on a deadfall and cleaned the bore of his Spencer. The fire made a splash of irregular light against the high rocks that sheltered them.

Saber leaned on a bedroll he'd never seen before and said: "Where did all of this come from?" He indicated the sleeping tarps, blankets, and small pile of supplies.

"Ed-John brought it out this morning in the buckboard. Lila baked us a pie." Burt said this with feeling, and Saber glanced at him pointedly, trying to read between the words.

"You know her long? She seems to be an unusual woman."

"Five years," Willie said. "Ever since her folks moved on Cardigan's place." He pulled the rabbit off the stick, and di-vided it onto three tin plates. "What's on for tonight?"

"A moonlight ride," Saber said. "Alone."

"You can get lost in those badlands," Burt said.

"I won't get lost," Saber said, and thought of Edith Bodry. He remembered her words and her smile and the feel of her as he lifted her from her horse. *She hates her husband,* he decided, *and a woman who hates will talk.* . . . He let his mind dwell on the possibilities as he settled back to eat.

Saber washed his plate with dirt, cleaning his knife and fork by plunging them into the ground. Darkness grew thicker, a chill breath blew down from the higher land, and he stood up to lay out his saddle blanket. Willie and Burt Kerry made an indistinct huddle on the other side of the fire. Saber licked a cigar into shape before speaking.

"How long have you known Missus Bodry, Willie?"

"Three . . . four years. Before she married Buck."

Saber phrased the question in his mind, then said: "There seems to be a little strain in the relationship . . . you know what I mean?"

"Buck is mean to her," Burt said. "Me and Hank Potter was foolin' around the back of Harris's stable one night when Buck and Edith came to get their rig. They was goin' 'round and 'round about somethin' when Buck just up and whacked her across the chops."

"She's his wife," Willie said. "And a man's wife is his business."

The tip of Saber's cigar glowed and died. He let the silence spread out, long and thin before murmuring: "I wonder why she puts up with it?"

"She married him for his money," Burt stated.

"You don't know that!" Willie's voice was sharp. "She ain't like that. She wanted security. I guess nobody's anyway blamin' her. Buck wasn't always that ornery."

Saber gave it some thought and said: "I wonder what changed the man?"

"Who knows?" Willie murmured. "Life's a funny proposition. A man thinks one way one day, and then tomorrow

69

comes along and changes it." He stretched out on his blankets. "Think I'll get a little sleep."

Saber let the night wear on until the moon was fifteen degrees up on the horizon, then rose to saddle the bay.

Burt rolled over in his blankets and said: "I can go with you if you like."

"Not tonight," Saber said, and pulled the cinch tight. He dropped the stirrups, and swung up. The fire had died to a small point of red. He turned the horse, sifting his way out of the rocks.

He crossed the fence, pausing to listen, but heard nothing save the small movements of nocturnal creatures. He let the horse walk, turning his head often until he approached the grove of trees. He studied their black length, seeing nothing, then dismounted and tethered the bay a few yards from the fringe. He hunkered down to wait, not really expecting her, but filled with a faint hope.

An hour passed. He fidgeted, wanting to roll a smoke. The moon was blanketed by moving clouds. He stood up as he heard the soft footfall of a horse on the grass, then he saw Edith threading her way along the edge of the trees. He stepped out to meet her.

Saber raised his arms for her to dismount, and she touched the ground, coming against him immediately.

She said huskily: "This is . . . insane."

"Then why did you come?"

She smiled at the foolishness of his question, knowing it was something he knew but still desired to hear, and laid her head against him, saying: "From the first moment I saw you . . . yesterday, on the road . . . you knew that I would come to you whenever you lifted a finger."

Her honesty struck a chord on his conscience, and he said

doubtfully: "Maybe this was not wise, after all."

"I wanted to come," she said quickly. "Buckley is asleep. It was easy for me to slip away."

She raised her head to look at him, and their lips met. He had intended that it be a casual kiss, but the fire within her ate into him, and he found his arms crushing her, holding her as if he would never get his fill.

She moaned softly as he released her, and she lay limply in his arms. "Is it so wicked to love you like this?"

Saber said gravely: "I should never have suggested this. You deserve better than I am."

"What are you, John?"

"You know my name, then?" Saber was surprised.

"A woman can learn what she wants to learn," Edith said. "She can also know when another man is out to get her husband."

"I hold Bodry no ill will."

"The badge on the lining of your coat is hard, John. What else could you be after?"

Saber's voice was slightly ragged. Her body was warm and sweetly curved against him, and her nearness unsteadied him. "You admit, then, that he is behind the missing cattle?"

"Is that what you want me to tell you? I could tell you, John. Then there would be no doubt in your mind. I know you now, and I know Buckley. There is no halfway with you . . . with a woman or a man you mean to get. You'd face Buckley straight out, and maybe Stiles and the rest of them. Then Buckley would be dead . . . oh, I have no doubt that you could kill him . . . then there would be just you and I to face each other and both know that that's the way we wanted it. You might love me then, and people would look at both of us, and they'd say that John Saber killed my husband so that he could have me for himself. I can tell you now about the cattle, if that's what you want."

She had touched the core of the thing like a fine rifle shot, and John Saber admired her for it.

"No," he said quietly, "don't tell me. I'll find it out for myself . . . one way or another."

"Then what of us, John?"

"I don't know," he said. "I wasn't thinking of tomorrow . . . only now."

"Perhaps that is wisest," Edith whispered, and raised her face for his kiss.

It was after midnight when Saber swung on the bay to make his way cautiously toward the Cardigan fence. The moon was a dying thing, on the downward swing, and fleeting clouds made the night black for long moments at a time.

He paused at the fence line, rolling a badly needed smoke, and tried to organize his thoughts. He had fallen in deeper than he'd intended, but he felt no regret. Her kisses had been a strong wine, drugging him, and now, as he tried to review their conversation with his usual detached air, it failed to come off as successfully as it had in the past.

He drew long on his smoke, cupping it between his hands, then raised his head as the soft drumming of hoofs came to him—a fast-ridden horse headed for the badlands to the west of him.

He heard a footfall behind him, and whirled as Willie Kerry said: "I've heard that horse before . . . on other nights like this."

"You walk like an Indian," Saber said, then concentrated on the distant sound. "Know that rider?"

"No," Kerry said. "Did you find out anything?"

Saber paused for a moment, then said: "Not much." He

made a decision. "Get your horse and we'll see where this fella's going."

Kerry swung away, reappearing a moment later with his pony. He mounted, waited for Saber to do likewise, then moved ahead through the fence, leading the way toward the badlands.

Within an hour the contours of the land began to change. Vegetation was sparse, and rocks made dark jumbled masses as they ran into jagged piles, the residue of some glacial push.

Kerry threaded his way expertly, silently upward, pausing in a scooped-out bowl to give the pony a breather. "Runs for miles like this," he said softly. "There's a few seeps, an' a line cabin over there to the north. If a man was to live out here, he'd probably use it."

"Bodry keep a crew out here?"

"Eight or ten men all the time," Kerry said. "I never saw 'em to count, but I can guess from the amount of grub that leaves the main ranch house."

"Let's go take a look."

"Pretty risky," Kerry said. "Better wait till daylight. We might stumble on more than we can handle."

"Night covers many things," Saber opined, and nudged his horse into motion.

The land climbed higher, and Saber struggled to keep from losing his sense of direction. He heard no sound except the ring of the bay's shod hoofs, saw nothing except the jumbled boulders and the black shadows that kept them company.

Kerry moved his pony to side Saber and pointed to a split in the ridge, yet a quarter mile distant. "There's the pass to the line cabin. My guess is there's a man with a rifle sittin' there, just waitin' for a couple of suckers to come snoopin' along."

"A valley in there?" Saber asked.

"Small one, but big enough, if you know what I mean."

Saber dismounted. "Let's take a look." He swung back his head to study the sky. "Be dawn in another hour and a half. We'll have time to take a quick look and get out."

Kerry led the horses away, snaking his Winchester from the rifle boot before he rejoined Saber. Then Willie moved out, taking care to keep rock shelter between them and the pass. He stopped a short time later to take his bearings, then moved off again, slightly to the left. They skirted the split rocks that announced the pass and climbed until it lay below them.

Saber stretched himself flat to study the land below. The moon peeked from behind the clouds, showing him the dark shape hunkered down below them in the pass. He nudged Kerry, drawing his attention to the man.

Kerry whispered: "He could be a real hindrance if we had to get out in a hurry."

"Can you do anything about it?"

Kerry smiled broadly. He stripped off his shell belt, stuffing the long-barreled .44 in the waistband of his jeans.

"See you later," he whispered, and was immediately swallowed by the night.

III

Saber listened carefully, but could hear no sound. No animal moved—nothing broke the silence. Below him, Kerry slipped like a shadow, and, farther down, the guard lay dozing over his rifle. Saber heard the sudden rattle of rocks, then a *thud,* followed by a long silence. He rubbed his hands together nervously and settled himself to wait, jumping in surprise as Willie Kerry materialized by his side.

"Done," Kerry said, and Saber stood up, ready to move down into the valley.

"I'd hate to have you after me," Saber said.

The dawn was just below the horizon and a faint light was beginning to dim the dying moon. Saber saw the cabin and pole corral ahead of him, a dim, squat shape.

Kerry said: "Get your look over with. They'll be up soon, and it ain't long to daylight."

Saber moved closer until he was twenty yards from the cabin. Inside, a stove lid *banged,* and a moment later a trickle of smoke oozed sluggishly from the chimney.

The land was rapidly turning gray with growing light, and a horse stamped nervously in the corral. A mile away, where grass covered the valley floor, a cattle herd stirred in isolated patches. Saber studied it for a long moment.

Willie touched him, whispering: "All right, you saw it. Now let's get out of here."

Saber laid a hand on Kerry's arm. "Stay here with that rifle. I'm going down and see how many're here." He moved away quickly, letting himself down to the level of the corral in the rear of the cabin. No window showed on that side. Saber skirted the pole enclosure, coming out against the log wall.

Voices came from within. A man's cursing was a long, hard rumble. The stove lid *banged* again, and Saber slid around the corner to a small window. He took off his hat, raising his head cautiously to peer in. He pulled his head back quickly as the front door opened and a tall, loosely built man rocked on the threshold. Ten feet and the building's corner separated them. Saber slipped the Colt from his shoulder holster.

Someone within yelled—"Lurch!"—and the man turned.

Saber peered around the corner again as the man named Lurch stepped clear of the cabin. He crossed to a stone watering trough, doused his head in the water, then stood sputtering and coughing as he dried his face. There was a gun tucked in the waistband of his trousers. He turned suddenly to toss the towel aside, saw Saber standing, bold and unprotected, by the building's corner.

There was enough light for Saber to see the surprise well up in Lurch's eyes, and then Lurch reached for his gun. John Saber shot him dead where he stood. The cabin came alive then, and, above him, Willie Kerry's .45-70 split the morning air. Heavy bullets thudded into the door, breaking a small window. Saber ran back of the cabin toward the corral. He kicked the pole gate out and entered, shouting at the milling horses, driving them out with rapid blasts of his gun.

The heavy rifle bang added to the pandemonium. Saber paused long enough in his flight for the safety of the rocks to fling the remaining loads in his gun at the window that blinked in the first rays of the rising sun.

He met Kerry as the boy scrambled from his concealment. Kerry said: "By hell . . . you like excitement, don't you?"

Saber shot the boy an irritated glance and moved out rapidly, keeping low, listening to the shouting and futile shots behind them. He thumbed fresh loads into his gun as he ran, pausing to give their back trail a sharp scrutiny. Shadows languished in the early light, the sun standing above the horizon, dead ahead of them.

"Good thing," Willie Kerry panted as he ran. "It will blind them so they can't see us good."

Saber saw the crumpled figure of the guard below him as they angled off toward the horses tethered in the rocks.

Burt Kerry sat on a deadfall, talking to Lila and Wes Cardigan as Willie Kerry and Saber crossed the fence below them. Willie Kerry's pony was lathered, and the livery bay stood quivering and blowing. Saber stamped to ease the stiffness in his legs, crossed to the fire to pour some coffee for himself. Tired lines rimmed his eyes, and there was a pinched look at the edge of his lips, not due entirely to fatigue. He sloshed the grounds around in the bottom of the cup, and drained the hot liquid without stopping.

"Well," Wes said, "what happened?"

"I've done a foolish thing, perhaps," Saber answered. "We heard a rider heading for the badlands around midnight and followed him. We found the cattle all right, but there was some shooting. I shot Lurch."

Lila pulled in her breath sharply, and gave her husband a quick glance. "Bad?" she asked.

"I'm afraid he's dead," Saber answered. "I'm sorry, Wes, but I may have started the cattle war you wanted to avoid."

"Well," Wes said finally, "I guess it had to come sooner or later. But I'm sorry to see it." He turned from the fire, taking Lila by the arm, and they went to their horses. He mounted, then paused, saying: "What I rode out for was to tell you that Edith Bodry is at the ranch house. She wants to see you."

It was like the shock of a bullet to Saber, and he looked quickly at Lila, but her smooth face told him nothing. He dropped his eyes and said—"I'll come in right away."—and turned toward his horse.

Burt Kerry stood and motioned toward his calico. "Fresher," he said, and watched Saber mount and ride off with the Cardigans.

The silence stretched out between the three, long and

thin, until Lila said: "It seems strange she would want to see you, doesn't it?"

"No," Saber said quietly. "We met and talked last night."

"Oh," Lila said.

Saber shot her a quick glance. "You think it was unwise . . . well, so do I," he said defensively.

"Who can say?" Lila pulled her horse back until she rode close to Saber. When she spoke again, her voice was soft and intense. "Listen to me, John. She has lived in hell these last six months. Whatever Bodry's reasons have been for treating her as he does are not important now, but what you intend to do about it is important."

"I've never before broken up a man's home."

Lila said: "I've seen the marks he has left on her. She would never leave him because she made a bargain, and she'll stick to it. But if a man loved her enough, he'd take her away from him, regardless."

Saber's only response was—"I'm sorry."—and he pulled his horse up beside Wes Cardigan's.

Buck Bodry's buckboard was parked by the barn. Edith Bodry paced the front porch in nervous agitation. She stopped as she saw Saber and the others dismount. Lila and Wes Cardigan moved on past her to enter the house. Edith's oval face was drawn as she clutched Saber's arm. She said tensely: "Ernie Stiles knows I met you last night. He heard me leave the ranch and followed. He was waiting for me at the far edge of the timber."

Saber drew on his self-control and asked: "What did he say?"

Edith colored as she told him: "He said to tell you to get out of the country before he told Buckley."

"You can't live with a threat hanging over your head."

"I know Stiles," Edith said. "He can keep a secret just so long . . . and then it will be bunkhouse gossip. You'll have to leave right away, John."

"You leave, Edith. Go away somewhere and I'll come to you as soon as this is over. Bodry won't do anything because I'll have him in jail."

"You're searching for a way out, John," Edith said, "and there isn't any. I've searched before, but the answer is always the same. I made a bargain . . . a foolish one, perhaps . . . because I lacked the courage to live in discomfort. Whatever happiness I have in my life, there'll always be that to remind me. I can't erase it. You can't erase it for me."

Saber's face was severe as he said softly: "All right, Edith . . . I'll leave."

"The compromise is hard for you, isn't it? You aren't accustomed to making them like I am."

"How would you know about me?" Saber asked.

"It isn't hard to find out about you, John . . . you've left a wide path." She smiled. "Men talk and women listen . . . that's the way it's been since time began . . . and then they wonder why a woman is sometimes wise."

"I could go to Bodry . . . talk to him. He would listen to me."

"Do you really believe that?"

"No, I'm just talking again," Saber said. He glanced at the buckboard and asked: "How did you get away?"

"I said I was going to town. Ernie Stiles is with me, waiting at the fork in the road. I can go anywhere as long as Ernie is with me." She drew a deep breath and added: "I suppose this is good bye . . . it's the best way, believe me."

"I don't believe you," Saber said.

Saber watched as she left the yard, the wheels churning a

long column of dust behind her, then he turned and entered the house. He went to his room and sat numbly on the bed, studying the design of the rug. It was not hard for him to acknowledge the fact that he loved her. It was the disillusionment with himself that rankled. He had thought himself above the petty mistakes that complicate men's lives—he had believed himself able to control his emotions, but now he knew that he had been fooling himself.

The door opened on the heels of a soft knock, and Lila closed it behind her, leaning against it.

"Another impropriety," Saber said wryly. "Wes will probably shoot me for this."

"Don't be silly. Wes knows where my love lies," Lila said. "The point is . . . do you know where yours is?"

Saber's mouth pulled into a severe line, and he said sharply: "You've read me ever since I arrived. You've called the shots. What will I do next?"

"Leave," Lila said. "If you were less proud, less haughty, you'd stay and finish what you've started."

"That's easy for you to say, isn't it?"

"No," Lila said quietly. "It isn't easy. Nothing in this world is easy. Do you think Buck Bodry will stay blind? Do you think you will ever find food again that won't taste like sawdust, a blanket that will be warm enough, or a sleep that isn't filled with dreams . . . if you leave like this?" Lila opened the door. "You have lived a long time without paying, and now you're finding out what it costs to be human. Edith knows . . . she found that out when she married Bodry." She left him then, closing the door softly behind her.

He waited a moment, then went into the hall and let himself out of the house. He crossed to the corral and found Wes Cardigan watching a colt frisk around the enclosure.

"Lend me a horse, Wes?"

Cardigan said: "Take your pick."

There was a question in Cardigan's eyes, but Saber didn't answer it as he cut out a rangy piebald and threw on a saddle. He adjusted the stirrups to suit him, and mounted heavily.

Cardigan crossed to him and stuck out his hand. "Best of luck, John."

"Mine has run out," Saber said. He lifted the reins as if to move out, then added: "Look after Edith, will you?"

"Stay," Cardigan said, "and look out for her yourself. That's what she wants."

"No," Saber said. "The price is too high." He nudged the horse with his heels and trotted from the yard.

Hondo, as Saber's horse paced the dust of Comanche Street, held the same feeling for him as when he had first seen it. It seemed unchanged. Even the horses looked the same, standing before the hitch rails. He saw Bodry's buckboard before Rutherford's store, the red-headed Stiles making a tall shadow as he leaned against the wall. Saber had every intention of riding past, but something within him gave way, and he felt his anger mounting. He stopped the horse, dismounted, and crossed to the hitch rail.

Ernie Stiles came alert, pushing himself away from the wall.

Saber placed his hands on the horizontal bar of the rack. "I should have killed you the other day, Stiles. I killed your pal, Lurch, this morning."

Stiles's eyes widened with disbelief.

Saber grinned wickedly. "You're not going to live to tell Buck Bodry anything."

"The hell you say!" Stiles yelled. He glanced around him to see what attention his voice had attracted. Three men, lounging in front of Keno Charlie's, were looking, and Edith

Bodry appeared in the door of the store.

"You played around with a man's wife, then tried to deny it when I faced you with it."

Edith covered her face with her hands and wheeled back into the store.

Stiles grinned and said: "All right, Saber. I got something to settle with you. You'll stay and face Bodry now because you got pride . . . and the whole town'll know about you and Edith inside an hour."

Stiles's hand rose to the lapel of his brush jacket, and paused.

Saber said—"I've never killed a man for pleasure before."—and reached for his gun. He drew smoothly but rapidly, cocking as the gun swung in front of him. He had Stiles beat and knew it. His bullet slammed carelessly into the man's chest. Stiles's gun went off at his feet, sending up a long splinter of wood, and he fell back, clawing at himself.

Boots pounded on the walk as people charged from open doorways. A man shoved his way through the gathering ring and asked: "What's goin' on here? I'm the sheriff of this county!"

Saber slid his badge into view. "I'm a federal officer, and this man was in my custody. He resisted arrest." He felt a momentary shame for hiding behind his badge, and then announced: "This man, in the company of Buckley Bodry, has been engaged in a large-scale rustling activity. I want a warrant issued for Bodry's arrest."

"You got proof?" the sheriff asked bluntly.

"Myself and Willie Kerry uncovered their hide-out on Bodry's property this morning. Jules Lurch was killed. That's all the proof I need."

A man detached himself from the gathering crowd, touched the sheriff, and they drew aside, the man whispering and pointing to the dead Stiles. The sheriff gave Saber a narrowed glance and said: "I don't think I'll issue any warrant."

Saber felt the blood mount in his face. He nodded curtly, and turned to shoulder his way into Rutherford's store. Edith Bodry stood by the dry goods counter, and Saber crossed to her. "I'm sorry," he said, "but it's out now."

"I heard him yelling," Edith said softly.

"Would it help if I told you that I love you too much ever to leave you?"

"That makes anything endurable," Edith said, and turned as Saber took her arm.

He pushed through the crowd roughly, leading her to the buckboard. He crossed to get Cardigan's horse, tied the reins to the rear, and mounted the seat beside her. He clucked to the team, and they wheeled out of town.

They let the silence build up between them, and then she asked: "Where are you taking me?"

"To Cardigan's," Saber said. "Then I'm going to Bodry."

"No!" Edith cried. "He'll be wild. Someone will be sure to ride out from town and tell him. He has Bill Dent by his side always. You won't have a chance with them."

"The man is a rustler . . . a thief. My primary concern is to effect his arrest."

"Of course," Edith said, remembering. She understood suddenly what a sacrifice this was to his pride, what a blow to his self-sufficiency that had always held him above other men, and she smiled sadly.

The Cardigan Ranch loomed in the distance. Edith said: "Before . . . I always hated the silence, but now it pleases me."

Saber nodded. "I hope always to please you."

He turned into the yard as Lila stepped onto the porch.

She stared at them in amazement, then gave him a broad smile.

Saber helped Edith step down, and Lila said to Saber: "I think I like you better."

"For myself," Saber asked, "or my weaknesses?"

"Both," Lila said, and led the way into the house.

Wes frowned slightly as he saw them, and motioned to Saber with his hand. "What made you change your mind?"

"I don't even know myself," Saber said. "I killed Stiles in town. Now, I'm going to Bodry's."

"Not alone," Cardigan said grimly. He stepped into the bedroom for his gun.

They rode to the fence line, waved to the Kerry boys, and waited until they came out of the rocks. "I want to make an arrest," Saber said. "Remember that, and we'll try to do it without shooting."

Burt and Willie nodded.

Cardigan brushed his mustache with a forefinger. "That," he said, "might take some doing."

Saber didn't reply, but lifted his reins and led the way across the Leaning Seven range.

They passed the grove of trees, and Saber gave it a long study, as if he should find something there that he had missed before. The sun had swung and was now on a downward arc, but still high enough to be hot. Sweat stained Saber's shirt, and he removed his coat, rolling it carefully. Willie Kerry glanced at the upside-down holster, but said nothing. No one spoke until Bodry's ranch house loomed, large and unpainted, before them.

Willie Kerry looked at Saber and asked: "You still mean to do this without shootin'?"

"Yes."

"What's the difference, if you kill him or the law kills him? He'll be dead."

"It would make a difference to me," Saber replied.

Willie sent a long, searching glance his way but said nothing more.

Bodry sat on the porch, the stocky Dent beside him. Saber dismounted by the watering trough. Cardigan and the Kerry boys remained mounted. Willie Kerry had shifted his .44 conveniently on his hip, and Burt laid his Spencer casually across the saddle.

Saber stopped with his foot on the bottom step of Bodry's porch. Bodry watched him with undisguised hatred.

"You've been a busy man since you got here," Bodry said. "You shot up my line shack, killed Lurch and Stiles, and run off with my wife. Look around and see if there's anything else you want."

"I'm placing you under arrest, Bodry, on the charge of cattle rustling."

Bodry stood up, rage crowding into his face. Dent stepped away from the wall. "And I'm charging you with wife-stealin'!" Bodry shouted. "Now who's guilty?"

"Are you going to submit to proper authority?" Saber asked tightly.

"I don't submit to nothin'," Bodry said. "You got all men tallied in that mind of yours, ain't you? Well, you got a lot to learn. A man ain't born mean or greedy . . . it's people that make him like that. You think I'm mean to Edith 'cause I hate her? Well, I don't. You don't know what it's like to get a woman, then find out she don't love you. It can change a man."

"You're under arrest," Saber repeated.

"No," Bodry said. "Ten years ago I'd probably have come along peaceful, but now I'd rather try my luck one more time." His hand made a dull slap as he hit his holster, pulling his gun.

Saber stood motionless, making no move to draw his weapon. Dent and Bodry moved together with great speed, but it seemed as though minutes passed before the muzzles cleared the lips of the holsters, as if they moved stiffly in a deep dream. Dent's gun leveled, as did Bodry's, and, behind Saber, Cardigan's shot blended with the report of Willie Kerry's .44.

Dent went backward, driven off the porch by Cardigan's bullet. Bodry braced himself on the railing, trying for a shot he never got off. Saber saw the bewildered expression on Bodry's face as he let out a long sigh and slid down. Voices cried out, and the Spencer let out a hoarse cough, and the yelling subsided.

Burt Kerry raised a young voice and called: "Come out of that cook shack with your hands up!"

They filed out, sullen-faced. Saber asked Cardigan: "Do you want to press charges?"

"No," Cardigan said. "Let Burt and Willie drive my beef back, and they can go to the devil." He slid his revolver back in its holster, and asked: "Coming, John?"

Saber considered it a long moment. He knew now that his understanding of men had been cursory, incomplete. There were no rules, no iron-clad forms in which to place men and have them fit. He saw Bodry as lawless, but now he understood that lawlessness. Most of all he understood himself. He was at best like the others, and it kicked at the foundation of his pride. He knew now that he had never walked above other men, but in the same dirt as they.

"No," Saber said. "I'll stay here. Send Edith home with Ed-John, will you?"

"Sure," Cardigan said, and smiled.

Saber looked at Willie Kerry then, and saw that there was no boldness, no arrogance in the boy's face. Worry had as yet failed to line it, and the down of adolescence still clung to his cheeks, but a man's eyes looked back at him. He stepped close to Willie's horse, and lifted his hand. Willie took it solemnly. "You knew I couldn't kill him, didn't you?"

Willie said: "I knew it." He wheeled his horse, and he and Burt and Cardigan rode from the yard.

Saber watched them until they became three small dots on the sea of burned grass. The expression on Willie's face remained with him. Kerry was a Texas man, but the killing had not touched him, had not colored his life one iota.

He's more of a man than I am, Saber thought. He realized then that he could face the townspeople and their talk, and this new knowledge of himself gave him heart. He settled himself on the porch, waiting for Edith to come home.

The Range That Hell Forgot

I

The sun had just completed its golden arc toward the western rim of the land when Willie Kerry stepped from the open door of Nusbaum's barbershop, cast a careful glance along the sprawled strip of loose dust that was Hondo's main street, then walked diagonally across it to enter Keno Charlie's saloon.

It was one of those summer evenings when the cool breath of a sage-scented breeze made a soothing interruption to the scorching heat of the desert's edge. On the south rim of the town a man yelled, and cattle lowed by the Texas Pacific loading pens. Toward the residences, a church bell sent up a melodious call, beckoning the gentry to an early worship. Willie halted on the gallery, hearing these sounds, soothed by them, and filled with a sense of peace that had been absent when he entered town two hours before.

Keno Charlie's was mildly crowded at this hour. A group of ranchers from the desert's edge made a clannish knot at the far end of the long bar. Frock-coated townsmen were mixing business with friendly drinking.

Willie eased himself in beside a tall, blond man with a sweeping mustache and wiggled his finger for his customary beer. Keno Charlie mopped his streaming face, sliding the schooner before him. Willie drank with a deep satisfaction.

The blond man smiled faintly. "How are things on Pewter Creek, Willie . . . a little dry?"

"Could stand some rain," Willie acknowledged, setting the beer down. He was a tall man, touching thirty, and hard work had hardened him. The loneliness of the land had worked on him until he carried a half-severe expression around a normally tolerant mouth. "Shipping much this fall, John?"

"Eight hundred head," John Saber said. "Market's down, and I want to hold them over on winter feed and ship next year."

Willie shook his head in mock sadness. "You big money cattleman . . . if I had eight hundred head, I'd be rich." He finished his beer, and turned to hook his elbows on the edge of the bar and survey the room. His jeans and brush jacket were patched and faded, still carrying the wrinkles of the clothesline.

Saber noticed this and remarked: "Dance tonight over at the Masonic Hall . . . or had you heard about it?"

"I heard," Willie said, and lapsed into silence.

Saber grinned behind his mustache. "When I was a kid back in Tennessee, I used to have a Redbone hound . . . damnedest dog you ever saw. All the time wanting something he couldn't have. I remember the time when that fool dog went all the way over into Arkansas after a Walker he took a fancy to. That dog never did amount to much . . . couldn't settle down and realize he was getting out of his class all the time."

Willie stiffened and kicked his temper into place. "You're a friend of mine, John. You can say it plainer than that and get away with it."

Saber licked a cigar into shape with great care. "That

desert bunch is a strange lot, son. This time you've got your sights set 'way too high." He held up a hand as Willie tried to interrupt. "Louise Dulane is a beauty, I'll admit that, but old Jesse's got his back humped against you. You're just asking for trouble by playing around with her. You're foolish to think otherwise."

Willie shoved himself away from the bar. "Some men are just naturally born fools." He pulled his battered hat at a rakish angle and sauntered from the saloon.

Long, black shadows lay between the close-set buildings. Buggies were wheeling into town. They pulled into the lot to the rear of the courtyard, parking in a solid row by the west side of the Masonic Hall. Willie watched this with a studied casualness, coming stiffly alert as three riders boiled into Hondo from the east. They nodded curtly as they trotted by, lean and saddle-pounded, a large anchor brand blazoned on their horses' flanks. He watched them dismount in the archway of the stable and waited as they crossed the street toward him. He was all caution but masked it behind the casual motions of his blunt fingers as he fashioned a cigarette. Lamplight now threw strong fingers of pale light onto the street. The three riders stopped near the bottom step.

Willie lifted his head as one of them spoke: "Long way from home, ain't you?" He had a flat, bold face, and he stared at Willie with a naked brazenness.

"Just in to dance with the pretty girls," Willie told him.

They stood there in a solid knot—Strang, Pecos, and Valverde.

Strang said: "Be careful who you dance with, Kerry."

Willie's eyebrows lifted belligerently. "You pickin' 'em for me?"

"Maybe," Strang said. He mounted the steps, Valverde

90

and Pecos at his heels. Willie waited until the swinging doors blocked them from his view, then moved off the porch. Music filtered out from the Masonic Hall as the musicians struck up a ragged chord, and Willie walked toward the gaunt figure lounging in the shadows of Keno Charlie's saloon.

A match flared with a sudden brightness, and George Rudy advised: "Watch out for those three."

"I'm not blind," Willie Kerry told him. He looked up and down the street. A half block away, Loyal Surrency and his wife rounded the corner of the Opera House, the woman turning to speak to the girl behind her. Her soft laugh came to Kerry, a melodious, ringing note, and he glanced at Rudy swathed in the shadows.

There was a rigid expectancy in the tall man, a searching in his pale eyes as the trio drew nearer. As they came abreast, a lamp was lighted in Keno Charlie's, and Rudy and Kerry were no longer hidden by the night. Loyal Surrency's head swung around quickly. The girl's laughter died, and she studied Rudy in frank appraisal until her mother nudged her. Surrency's voice was even, with no hint of friendliness when he said: " 'Evening, Kerry." He gave George Rudy a curt nod.

They moved on.

Kerry studied Rudy's face as he followed Marilee Surrency with his eyes. Then Kerry dropped his gaze quickly, somehow feeling that he was intruding. Rudy's cigar lay dead between his long fingers. He smiled wanly. "Even in Hondo we have a dividing line."

"I didn't know it included piano players," Kerry said.

Rudy applied another match to his cigar. The light shone on his embroidered vest and white silk shirt. He whipped the match out. "Surrency isn't tone deaf. In fact, he comes into Keno Charlie's often to hear me play Chopin and Beethoven, in off hours. However, he has an aversion to my sitting in his parlor to play for his daughter. My place is in the saloon. That was established the first evening I tried to call."

"This is a free country," Willie maintained. "A man can take what he wants . . . and earns."

"Is that what you have in mind?"

"Maybe," Willie admitted. "When I get ready."

"You're very elemental," Rudy said admiringly. "Unfortunately I am a thinker . . . prone to lengthy mental dissertation. I've wondered if a girl like Marilee . . . or Louise . . . could take it. Suddenly finding themselves without luxuries, I mean."

"One way to find out," Willie murmured.

"A serious step," Rudy counseled. "And if you found out you'd made a mistake, how would you correct it?"

"Never gave it much thought," Willie said, and stepped from Keno Charlie's porch. A block away, the band swung into "Dixie," announcing the beginning of the dance. Willie paused to listen for a moment, then asked Rudy: "Comin' over?"

"Later, perhaps," Rudy said, and turned back into the saloon.

Willie crossed to the other side of the street and walked toward the hall. The building was ablaze with light and colored Japanese lanterns. Dancers made a bobbing mass on the cleared floor, and Willie paused in the doorway to watch them. The music pulsed, a deep throbbing beneath the noise of capering feet and laughing women.

Sam Harms's bulk half blocked the door as Willie shouldered past him. He touched the young man on the arm. "No trouble tonight now, Willie." Harms was all stomach beneath the star pinned to his parted vest.

"I just came to have a good time," Willie said, brushing

92

past. He crossed to the west wall, halting near the fringe of the stag line. He saw Saber in the middle of the floor, dancing with his wife, and searched the crowd until he found Strang and Pecos in a far corner. Willie stared at them for a long moment, until their heads came up, then he moved onto the floor toward Louise Dulane.

Valverde swung her wide as Kerry stepped quickly between them to take her hand and whirl her among the other dancers. She gave Kerry that puzzling half smile when he looked at her. Her smooth shoulders rose, round and bare, from her billowing white gown. She was a full-breasted girl, with skin gleaming like pale ivory in the lamplight. Her dark eyes glowed from the piquant frame of her face. Her lustrous brown hair was coiled high on her head.

Willie murmured: "I don't guess I ever seen you look prettier."

She flushed beneath his candid gaze. "I don't think you've ever done anything more foolish. Valverde will settle this before the night's over."

He pulled her against him and laughed, a joy and a recklessness blending within him. This night had no end for him. No danger was as real as the girl in his arms. He came to the side door and wheeled her toward it. Then they were outside with the clear night around them, shadows bathing them.

Louise didn't pull away from the arm that encircled her waist. "This is insane, Willie. Father will be furious." Her voice said one thing while her tone told him something else.

Willie Kerry laughed, and kissed her. She surrendered to him, answering him with the pressure of her arms. Kerry drew away, and pulled in a ragged breath. He took her arm, and led her back to the hall.

"I'm sure in the mood for dancin'," he told her, and

whirled her blithely away to the beat of the music.

They threaded their way among the dancing couples. Willie ignored Jesse Dulane's heavy-browed scowl. Valverde had taken a place along the wall, shoving himself away as the music stopped. People eddied around them. Marilee Surrency brushed by him with a quick smile, and passed on.

Louise Dulane gripped Willie's arm tightly as Valverde broke off a conversation with her father and shuffled through the crowd toward them. Sam Harms moved then, but Valverde had already stopped before Kerry. "That's my girl you're dancin' with." His voice was low, filled with that hushed tightness that carries below louder voices, bringing with it a ring of chopped silence.

Willie asked Louise: "Are you his girl?"

"No."

Willie's good humor faded. "Drag your picket then. If. . . ."

Sam Harms shoved his bulk between them, and pushed Valverde back with a stiffened arm. "Let's just have a nice, quiet time . . . shall we?"

Valverde wanted to make a fight of it, but he shot a glance at Jesse Dulane, and the old man shook his head imperceptibly. The squat rider mumbled under his breath, and moved away. Willie watched this with a quiet attention. Harms warned: "You better go, Willie. You're just pullin' the lion's tail."

"Sure," Willie agreed. He took Louise by the arm, leading her outside again. There was a haste in him then, the pressure of time against him. He blurted: "You know I love you, and I know you love me, too. Let's ride out of here and go to Wineglass and get married."

Louise made a vague motion toward her father.

Willie said: "I'm not marryin' him. I'm marryin' you! To

hell with his permission. You got to get away from him some-time."

She wanted to. He could see that. She opened her mouth, suddenly confused and said haltingly: "Willie, I. . . ."

"Fine," Willie said quickly. "I like a woman who can make up her mind." He took her hand then and led her from the porch, cutting across the lawn. Trees blocked out the faint night light, making the growth of sycamores a solid black-ness. Willie halted abruptly as a cigar glowed, and died.

John Saber stepped from the shadows and said softly: "So, you're going to do it anyway?"

Willie made no immediate answer.

Saber chuckled. "Take my rig, over at the livery stable. I'll rent one for Edith and me when we get ready to leave."

"Thank you," Louise said breathlessly, and they left the darkness to cross the street.

A solitary lantern hung in the stable's arch. Willie left her in the shadows while he hitched up Saber's team. He emerged a moment later, leading them, and handed her into the buggy. Comanche Street was bare when he turned out onto it. He drove toward the north road that led to his place in the badlands, whipping the team into a brisk trot as they passed the hall. There was a burst of excitement in the yard, a flurry of brief action, and the strident call: "Fight . . . fight! George Rudy's fightin' the banker!"

Lights and sound faded behind them. The night swal-lowed them as he tooled the team over the rutted road. He lis-tened to the clatter of the rig, the solid beat of the horses' hoofs, and pondered that call about a fight.

"What did it mean?" Louise asked.

"I don't know," Wes admitted. "George is about at the end of his rope. Love makes a man do foolish things."

"Does it make you do foolish things?"

Willie shot her a quick look and saw the smile on her face. "Your dad has about ten thousand dollars. I have less than twenty dollars, yet I want his daughter for a wife. Is that foolish?"

"Very," Louise told him, "but I love you for it." She fell silent then, letting the miles drift past them, letting the night wear on.

They climbed higher until the desert lay below them, white and stark in the faint moonlight. Three hours later they came to the fork in the road leading to Cardigan's Sunrise spread, the other to Saber's Leaning Seven, and beyond, in the badlands, the Broken Spur, Willie Kerry's one-man ranch.

The altitude lent a chill to the air, and Willie halted to throw a robe around her bare shoulders. An hour later they left the road as it cut toward Saber's ranch house, taking a winding course that twisted and slashed its way through rock and scrub pine.

It was after eleven when Willie pulled close to his cabin and dismounted, lifting Louise to the ground. She sagged against him for a moment.

He said: "This is as far as we can take the buggy. There's some of my brother's clothes in the cabin. You get into 'em and I'll saddle a couple of horses for us."

He pulled her against him then, and she came willingly, their lips meeting for a long moment. She was breathless when she broke away. He turned with her to enter and light the lamp.

She looked around at the peeled log walls, the sparse furniture. Willie saw this, and there was no apology in his voice. "A man can't start out a success." He turned from her then, stopping in the doorway to add—"Don't be long."—and moved off toward the barn at a long-legged lope.

The remainder of the night passed swiftly for them, a quick succession of events that, at dawn, led them toward the desert and Jesse Dulane's ranch. Wineglass was miles behind them, as was the wizened minister who had solemnized the affair. Louise slept in the saddle, her chin bobbing against her chest. Willie dismounted stiffly and lifted her to the ground. They were at the outer fringe of the timber, the desert slightly below and west of them. Dulane's Anchor spread squatted three miles away, now only an indistinct jumble of rough buildings.

Willie kindled a small fire, and boiled a pot of coffee.

"Louise." He touched her, bringing her awake and handed her the tin cup. She drank quickly, then handed it back to him, leaning back against the bole of a stunted tree.

"Please let me go in alone, Willie."

She watched his face, but he gave no sign that he had heard her. Willie drained the cup, kicked the fire until it was smothered with dirt, and then pulled her to her feet.

"You're not too tired?"

She shook her head as he helped her mount. They angled off the slope to hit the road a half hour later.

Dawn had blossomed into a full, sunny morning when they finally crossed the ranch yard. Men made a cursing group around the corral as horses were being cut out. Eyes swung to them, then turned back to the business at hand, as they dismounted a few yards from the porch.

Jesse Dulane came from the house, Strang and Valverde at his heels. He gave his daughter a close inspection, then said: "So you gone and done it? Well, I seen it comin', danged if I didn't. Headstrong, that's what you are . . . just like your mother, but I like a woman that way." He made a motion toward Strang with his head and said curtly: "Get on with the work."

Strang stepped off the porch.

Valverde moved to follow Strang, but Jesse laid a hand on his arm, holding him. "Not you," he said. "You got a grudge, and a man packin' a grudge ain't worth a damn to me or himself unless he gets it out of his system. You been wantin' to tangle with Kerry . . . all right, here's Kerry. Tangle with him."

Valverde made no attempt to hide his eagerness. He took a long step toward Kerry, only to be halted by the old man's voice.

"Take that danged gun off! I won't have you losin' your head and pluggin' my brand new son-in-law just because you got a nasty temper."

Valverde let the gun belt drop, and stepped from the porch only to be knocked into a sprawl by Kerry's driving fist.

Jesse snorted in disgust as Valverde struggled to his feet. "Hell," Jesse told him, "this ain't no waltz!"

Valverde's temper was a live thing, and he let it out, boring in with the ferocity of a wild animal. Willie withstood the brunt of the attack, then leveled the squat man with a damaging uppercut.

Louise grabbed her father's arm, shouting: "Stop them! Make them stop!"

"What for?" Jesse said. "Man was made to fight over a woman. It's as natural as the sun and the wind. Look at 'em go at it!"

Kerry took a slashing fist across the mouth to get near Valverde, then closed one of the man's eyes with a meaty hook. Valverde went down on one knee. Kerry stepped back, waiting for him to get up.

Jesse yelled: "Stomp him . . . stomp him!"

Kerry's breath was ragged, and he pulled for wind. "You . . . fight your . . . way. I'll fight him . . . mine."

Valverde made his feet then, picking up a fist-sized rock from the yard. Jesse shouted at him, but he ignored the old man, lifting his hand to strike. A gun blasted behind Kerry, and he jumped as Valverde bent over, clutching a bullet-creased hip. Jesse holstered his .38-40.

"Once," Jesse said, "I could have shot the danged thing outta his hand, but my eyes are goin' out on me, I guess." He gave Valverde a hard glance. "Git to the bunkhouse and have Cookie patch that up." The old man's face was hard, and his mouth, behind his ragged, gray mustache, was pulled into a thin line.

Willie Kerry pawed at his bruised mouth and looked at Jesse.

Louise said: "I'm married now, Father. I've come after my things."

"You're wearin' 'em," Jesse told her.

Louise took a backward step and gasped.

"Don't say I didn't tell you. You know how I feel about you marryin' some brush-popper. I wanted you to be a lady, but you prefer him. All right . . . start out that way, flat broke and standin' in the only clothes you wear."

"That's carrying bein' tough a little too far," Willie said.

"Is it now?" Jesse wanted to know. "I fed this young beauty on milk and honey . . . maybe she's a little soft. She's on her own now, and she made her bed. Let's see if she's woman enough to lie in it. She either has gumption or she ain't. Time will tell. I give her six months to come crawlin' back, and, when she does, don't ever come after her, 'cause she only gets one chance to come back."

"She'll never come back to you," Willie prophesied.

"Won't she, now?" Jesse taunted. "How long do you think you'll stay around when things start gettin' tough for you?"

"It finally comes out," Willie said tightly. "All right, confine the fight to me. Don't drag her into it." He took a ragged breath, trying to get control of his temper. "You make a big show of fightin' fair . . . what can you do to me unless you step outside the law?"

Jesse smiled, and waved them away with his hand. "Go on . . . go home with him. Go back to that hole in the wall and the loneliness and the empty bellies."

Louise stared at her father. "I don't think I ever knew you before. I think I sincerely hate you now."

A look of grief flitted across her father's eyes, then was gone.

Willie took Louise by the arm, leading her to the waiting horses, wondering about it. They mounted and rode from the yard.

II

The first month passed happily, but Willie felt the added pressure. He rode into the hills for three days, returning on the fourth, driving four raw-boned steers before him. He drove them into Hondo and sold them, buying her cloth and things for the house with the twenty-eight dollars. Louise made no complaint, even appeared happy, but he saw the faraway look in her eyes when she thought he wasn't looking. He felt the shoulder-shaking sobs in the night when she supposed him sound asleep beside her. Willie recognized a mistake when he made one, and he had the solution at his fingertips, but he lacked the will power to take her home, to put her away from him forever.

The supper hour passed, as had many others, with her

laughter filling the small room, her beauty a tonic after a hard day's work. Willie shoved his plate away from him and fashioned a smoke with great care. Louise watched him, then said: "Tell me about it, Willie. I think it would help both of us."

He was surprised but masked it quickly. "I don't know the words. I'm afraid I might use the wrong ones, and then I'd hurt you."

Her dark eyes glowed, and she said simply: "Just say the words. I'll know what meanings to attach to them."

There was a long silence, a thoughtful drawing on his cigarette, then: "I been wanting to talk to you about how it will be for us next year, our future here . . . but there won't be any future. Oh, I guess you love me, but love ain't enough, is it?"

She looked at him solemnly and said honestly: "I don't know, Willie. Most of the time it is, but, then again, I get lonely. I guess I'm not the kind of a woman who *likes* to be poor."

Willie sighed deeply and crossed to the door to throw out his cigarette. "I guess that sums it up all right," he said quietly, and went outside for a drink of water. He paused by the well curbing, hearing the night sounds around him. He was half turned to reënter the cabin, when the sheriff's voice said: " 'Evenin', Willie."

Kerry whirled, seeing them then in the darkness, the squat, blurred shapes of horses and riders. "Who's with you?" Willie forced his voice to be calm.

"Just Ron Banks, my deputy," Harms said, "and Strang, Pecos, and Valverde."

"What do you want?" Kerry asked.

Louise stepped to the door, standing framed in the lamplight.

"Get back in the house," Kerry told her, and the door closed.

"I got a writ here," Harms said. "We want to inspect your cattle for rustled stock."

Kerry snorted. "There ain't been no rustlin' around here since Saber cleaned Bodry's bunch out ten years ago. Besides, a man don't need no writ to look at another man's herd. What's behind all this?"

"I'm just doin' my job," Harms maintained. "Dulane thought, seein' how you and him is sorta on the outs, it would be better to have the court order."

"All right," Willie said shortly. "We'll start in the mornin'."

" 'Fraid not," Strang said. "The old man's gonna ship day after tomorrow 'n' he wants all he can get."

"What the devil!" Willie's temper threatened to get the better of him. "I've got on to sixty head in this brush. How the devil do you expect me to cut them out in time?"

"Gotta be done," Harms said. "Court order."

"I get it," Willie said. "He wants to see me work day and night, is that it?"

"Take it any way you want," Strang said. "Go get your horse and kiss your wife good bye for a few days."

Willie glowered at them in the darkness, then went into the house. He emerged ten minutes later, sullen and silent, and crossed to the barn.

He rode in on the morning of the third day, dirty, with a half-inch stubble on his face. Louise met him at the door. He spent ten minutes at the horse trough before slipping into clean clothes and putting his razor away. She had a meal ready for him, and he ate in silence. Louise waited until he lifted his coffee cup, then blurted: "I hate him . . . I hate him!"

Willie shook his head. "No, you know that isn't so. It's just that he's alone now, and I guess that can hurt when you get older."

"How many of his cattle did you find?"

"None. I knew there wouldn't be any, but I had to look." Willie scrubbed a hand across his face, and stood up. "I could sure use some sleep, but there's something I have to do in town. Guess I'd better get it done."

He smiled at her, but she shook her head, saying: "I'll wait here."

He went out to his horse then, wondering if she was ashamed to face her friends with only a homemade dress to show for her married life. Willie rode slowly from the yard.

He paused on the bluff overlooking Hondo. It was a sight he never tired of seeing, but, somehow, today it failed to raise his spirits. He nudged the horse with his heels, and an hour later came onto the main street. Buggies and buckboards were thick along the hitch racks, and it was only then that he realized it was Saturday. He passed the loading pens, noticing that they were empty. He felt an idea brush him and moved over to the agent's window to ask: "Jesse Dulane ship yesterday?"

The agent looked surprised. "Why, no, Willie. Beef prices dropped another quarter. He wouldn't ship now."

Willie nodded his thanks, and trotted the length of the street. Edith Saber called to him, and he swung his horse to dismount before her.

"Willie," she said, "John told me to ask you if you could spare some time. He wanted to put on another crew and needs a good boss. There's the extra house that goes in with the deal."

Willie read nothing in her voice, but he felt something

103

there. He lowered his head as though deep in thought, thinking: *It sure must show plain enough.* He looked up at her and murmured—"I'll think it over."—and tipped his hat, walking on down the street.

Loyal Surrency's bank door stood open. Willie walked in, nodded to the cashier, and swung the low mahogany gate aside to enter the inner office. Surrency sat behind his desk like an overgrown bullfrog. He glanced at Willie, and his eyes clouded, as though he had been reminded of something unpleasant.

Willie pulled a chair back and sat down.

Surrency said briefly: "What is it this time?"

Willie flushed. "This time? I only been in here once before and that was to get the loan in the first place."

"A little dry this year," Surrency said. "Heard you'd been having trouble."

Willie had no wish to discuss it and made a vague motion with his hand. "It comes and goes," he told the banker.

"Seen your friend, Rudy?"

"Why, no," Willie said, something in the man's voice turning him cautious.

"When are you going to be able to start paying again? You're three months behind now."

"I know that," Willie admitted. "I been waitin' for the beef market to climb just like everyone else. I mean to pay, but that isn't what I came in to talk about. I need a little ready cash . . . maybe fifty, seventy-five dollars. I'd kinda like to buy my wife a few things."

Surrency smiled then, and Kerry stiffened, knowing it to be a strange thing. Surrency put his beefy hands together and said, as if each word gave him great pleasure: "I've put a good deal of thought into your note, Kerry, and I've come to the conclusion that the best procedure would be foreclosure."

Kerry slapped the arms of his chair. "That's a little sudden, ain't it? You gave me a six months' extension on that note."

"I've changed my mind," Loyal Surrency said flatly.

"Mighty convenient, ain't it?"

"Just what do you mean?"

"I don't exactly know," Kerry admitted. "I'd like to know what the hell *you* mean."

"I had trouble with a man," Loyal said. "I feel that you're responsible." Kerry's face was puzzled, and Surrency supplied: "George Rudy. He took a fancy to my daughter. Naturally I objected, and I believe everything would have been all right if you hadn't seen fit to encourage him. You were talking to him the night of the dance, then you ran away with Dulane's daughter. The combination was sufficient to cause Rudy's unforgivable words to me."

"Wasn't there some kind of fight?" Willie asked pointedly.

Surrency's face was livid as he snapped: "Yes, dammit. The pup had the effrontery to demand satisfaction."

"I take it you got stomped?"

Surrency scowled, and Willie laughed. He felt he could afford to at this point.

Surrency said coldly: "Get your things together and move off that property, or I'll have the sheriff move you off."

"So Rudy licked you," Willie murmured. "You weren't the cut-proud bully boy you thought you were after all. What about Marilee? Did she cradle your fat head and tell you she'd never see the brute again, or was she woman enough to go with him?"

Surrency surged to his feet, pawing at Kerry. Willie's temper filled him. He stretched Loyal Surrency flat on his back with one punch.

There was a great thrashing sound from the other room as

the teller crowded through the door to pick up the banker. Surrency's mouth was bleeding, and he shook his fist at Kerry. "I'll have the sheriff after you for this!"

"Go to hell," Willie told him. He stalked out to stand on the boardwalk. He stood there letting his anger die and saw John Saber go into Keno Charlie's. Willie felt a whim nudge him and crossed the street.

III

Saber stood belly flat against the bar, and Kerry sided him. Saber shot him a quick glance and commented: "Hot today, isn't it?"

"Thanks for the job," Willie said, watching Saber's face.

The man was nimble-witted and an excellent poker player, but Willie caught the flitting puzzlement in his eyes before Saber lifted his beer and stated: "Think nothin' of it . . . nothing at all." He set the schooner down. "Have one." Willie shook his head, and Saber asked: "Wife object?"

"No," Willie said. "It don't seem right, somehow . . . me here havin' a beer and her home with one dress to her name. A homemade one at that."

Saber studied his reflection in the polished bar. "I know how it is."

The batwings *squeaked,* and heads turned. Jesse Dulane crossed to the far end of the bar. Willie straightened and walked over to him. Jesse took a beer from the bartender and said: "From the way you're walkin' stiff-legged, I can see you're just honin' for a tussle."

"Ain't I got a good reason?"

"Maybe you have," Jesse told him, "maybe you ain't. But it's too hot to wrassle or crack each other with our knuckles."

Saber lifted his drink and slid along the bar until he was within three feet of Willie. His voice was quiet, but the warning was there: "Back off, Willie."

Kerry turned his head quickly, not understanding this. "This is none of your damned business, John."

"You're mistaken," Saber told him. "This *is* my business. Come on back and have a beer before your hot head gets you into trouble."

Willie looked around the room, returning the stares, then followed Saber to the other end of the bar. He waited until the bartender drew another beer before he said softly: "I come because you got a reason. I know you'll tell me."

Saber let out a long breath. "Give Dulane a chance to know you. He just wants to find out what kind of a man you are."

"Hell," Willie said impatiently, "why don't he ask around? People here have known me for ten, twelve years."

"You know better than that," Saber pointed out. "A man doesn't take another man's word on those things. He finds out for himself. I told you once they were a clannish lot . . . give him a little time."

"All right." Willie sighed. "No bloodshed." He lapsed into silence for a moment, then said: "I don't see George Rudy around."

"Gone," Saber said. "Went to Dallas the morning after his fight with Loyal Surrency. Went to Surrency's house, big as life, and took the girl. I guess she was eager to go."

"That takes money."

"True," Saber agreed, "but he had some. Keno Charlie gave him three hundred to sweeten the pot." He leaned on the bar, and looked around the room. He stared thoughtfully at his hands for a long moment, then said: "Speakin' of money, I saw you come out of Loyal's bank. A little short?"

"I wanted to get Louise a few things," Willie said quietly.

"That's not good enough. If you needed it for anything but that, I'd let you have it, but she's got to start at the bottom if she wants to grow up."

Kerry stiffened and said in a brittle tone: "I've heard some rough talk lately. I don't want to hear any more . . . not even from you."

"Don't be a fool, Willie," Saber said explosively. "Can't you see what Jesse's doing?"

"No," Willie said hotly, "and I don't want to."

"Better come off the boil," Saber advised. "Losing your temper won't help anything."

"Wait a minute," Willie warned. "You and I have had some rough times together but that don't give you the right to stand back and pick my wife to pieces."

Saber drained his glass with a few quick swallows, and wiped the foam from his mouth with his handkerchief. He gave Willie a straight look—"Excuse my big mouth."—and walked out.

Willie Kerry drew an aimless design on the bar's wet surface with a blunt finger. The bartender came up to him and asked: "Want something?" Kerry shook his head and went outside to mount his horse.

Louise Kerry bent over the steaming tub. Willie carried wood for the fire. Clothes hung wetly from a lariat strung from the roof of the well cover to the far corner of the cabin. The heat lay heavy on the land, and her gingham dress was dark with sweat across the back and shoulders. Willie walked up behind her and held her hands from further rubbing on the board. "That's enough," he told her firmly. "Let the rest go dirty."

Her face was flushed from the heat, and her hair lay awry.

108

He crossed to the well to draw a bucket of cool water. They drank gratefully of its coolness. Finally they sat on the steps, close, but Willie had the distinct feeling they were growing apart. She let the silence spread out for a moment, then asked: "Why did you go into town?"

"Money."

"Are we broke?"

"No," Willie said, "but there were some things I wanted to buy for you."

"I have all I need," Louise said softly.

Willie looked at her, knowing she lied to save his pride. He sat with his head down and remained that way until she touched him gently on the knee. He raised his head in time to see three horsemen leave the rocks, angling toward the cabin. Willie stood up and went inside. When he came out, he was wearing his gun.

Strang, Pecos, and Valverde stopped twenty feet away. Strang said: "I never knew you to carry a gun, Kerry."

"Before your time," Kerry told him, and gave them a studied attention. Valverde shifted on his horse and gave Pecos a knowing look. Kerry caught this: "Say what you want, then drag it."

Strang stared at him. "Unfriendly cuss, ain't you?"

"Speak up or ride out!"

Strang chuckled deeply in his throat and looked at Louise. "Your pap wants to know if you've got a craw full yet."

Louise stiffened. "Is he getting impatient?"

Strang shook his head. "I wouldn't know, ma'am."

Willie felt his temper push at him, and Valverde said: "I can't get over it . . . you packin' a gun."

"Leave him alone," Strang warned. "We don't want trouble."

"Speak for yourself," Valverde told him. He leaned on the

109

saddle horn, staring at Kerry with a wide grin slashed across his face. "Is it for show, or do you really shoot it now and then?"

"Take it easy," Strang cautioned, not liking the expression on Willie's face. He gave Louise another pointed look and said: "You sure you won't change your mind?"

She shook her head, and Strang turned.

"Don't be in a hurry," Valverde said. "I want to see this fella shoot. Go ahead, bronc'-stomper . . . shoot."

"Get that big mouth outta here," Willie warned quietly.

Strang made a move toward Valverde, but the man reached across his stomach and casually drew his gun. Willie waited until the muzzle was swinging toward him, then pulled, spilling the squat man from the saddle with one quick shot. The echo bounded and rebounded through the hills. Willie advised: "Pick him up and get him out of here . . . you with him."

Strang and Pecos dismounted hurriedly and draped the groaning man across his horse. They mounted with no hostile move, and Strang said: "This isn't the first time you've smelled powder."

"And it won't be the last," Willie informed him.

He stood there and watched them ride out, then went into the cabin and hung up his gun. Louise watched him closely. Trouble crowded Willie until he no longer knew where he had made his first mistake.

He took her gently by the arms, pulling her to her feet. His voice was humble. "Louise, a man like me ain't nothin', but it takes something like this to make him see it. I'm guilty of loving you . . . I never should have done that, but it was something I couldn't help. I never should've brought you here, made a slave of you . . . not giving you anything but hard work and trouble. Your father was right . . . you belong with him and his money. I'll take you back."

"Have I nothing to say about it?"

"I guess," Willie told her, "that you're the sweetest thing in this world and you'd say a lot of things to save my pride. Well, it just ain't worth savin'. I'm gonna take you back."

"If you do," Louise said, "there will never be another chance."

"I don't deserve another chance." Willie went to the barn to hitch up his buckboard. Halfway there, he turned to look at her—slowly. . . .

Dulane's Anchor still looked the same to him as he watched it materialize from the ledge overlooking the desert, but somehow it seemed sharper, clearer. Willie glanced at Louise on the wagon seat, but her face was set, and she stared straight ahead, saying nothing. The silence had remained unbroken throughout the entire ride.

Willie rapped the horse, and they moved toward the loose cluster of buildings. Jesse Dulane sat on his wide porch, Strang on the steps before him like a faithful dog. They paced slowly into the yard. Finally Willie hopped down, and lifted his arms for Louise.

Jesse watched this with no change of expression.

Willie asked: "How is Valverde?"

Strang's eyes widened, and he said: "I'm surprised you asked. He'll be all right. Your bullet gouged out a helluva hunk of meat, but it'll grow back."

The answer satisfied Kerry. He looked at Jesse Dulane.

Dulane watched his daughter, noticed her work-roughened hands, the much-washed dress, and asked bluntly: "Get your belly full of hard work, back fat, and beans?"

"No," Louise said heatedly. "He just decided that I'm too good to be his wife."

"Ha!" Jesse said, and slapped his thigh. "He did, did he? Well, let me tell you something, Kerry. My wife and I came into this country thirty years ago with one cow, a horse, a Sharps rifle, and a lot of ambition. She lived hard, played hard, and, by God, we loved hard . . . but she was all woman . . . and my daughter's the same."

Louise gave Willie a long look and said: "Understand something before I walk in that door. I love you more than anything in this world, even my father. I felt homesick, yes, but it was a natural thing. I was proud of you, and I still am. But you aren't content to just have me love you. I never told you this, Willie, but I would have lain in the dirt and waited for you if you'd wanted me to."

She opened the door. Her father spoke sharply: "Remember what I said, girl! Set foot in that house now and you've given up . . . there ain't no turnin' back after that door closes."

"We'll see," Louise murmured, and went into the house.

Kerry stared after her, and Jesse Dulane chuckled. "It's all like a game of poker, sonny, but I won. You held all the cards, and I bluffed you out. I ain't no fool. I knowed I couldn't keep her forever, and I wanted her to have a man. You're a man, but you weren't quite man enough, or you'd never give her up. I played a poor hand right into a winner."

The screen door opened, and Louise stepped onto the porch, Jesse's double-barreled shotgun cradled in the crook of her arm. She pointed the twin bores at her father.

Jesse Dulane straightened and said: "Hey, be careful with that danged thing . . . it's loaded!"

"I know it," Louise said firmly. "You also taught me how to shoot it." Jesse started to stand up, but she motioned him down with the gun. "Get him a horse, Strang." The man got uncertainly to his feet, then moved off when he looked into her eyes.

"You're an old, hard-headed goat, and I love you, but this time one of your lessons is going to backfire in your face. You put me out with only the clothes on my back, trying to find out if I was a woman or not. You gave Willie hell to see if he was your kind of man. Well, now you can have some of your own medicine."

"You can't do this to me, honey! I own this place!"

"I hold a shotgun, and in Texas that's better than a fist full of deeds. I've heard you say so yourself!"

She glanced at Strang as he appeared with Jesse's pony. Louise motioned with the shotgun, and Jesse stood up wearily and crossed to the horse. He pulled himself up into the saddle with a grunt. There was a thinly veiled pride in his eyes as he looked at her. "Get going," Louise told him. "Ride until your pants fall to pieces, and, when Willie and I get ready, we'll send Strang after you, and you can come back. Swallowing your pride won't choke you . . . you'll find that out." She turned to Willie then and added: "This is your last chance too, buster. In the future, when I say I love you . . . I mean just that."

Jesse Dulane watched this with a thin grin spreading across his old face. He said: "Dammit, girl, if you was a son, I couldn't be prouder." He was laughing as he rode from the yard.

Willie understood it, then—his biggest mistake. He hadn't really shared anything with her, assuming the whole burden himself without considering her a part of it. He crossed to her, and put his arms around her. She smiled up at him. There was nothing about either of them that the other didn't understand now. Willie suddenly felt that they were solidified and made whole. It was a new feeling to him and perhaps to her—he had no way of knowing—but she was his woman, and she pleased him as nothing else ever had.

The Devil's Roundup

I

It was questionable whether the horse or the rider attracted the attention as he rode slowly down Hondo's main street. He had no saddle, just a moth-eaten blanket thrown over the horse's bony back, riding Indian fashion, hunched over with the scuffed toes of his half boots tucked inward. His shoulders, under the faded and much-patched brush jacket, were bunched up, still carrying the chill of the high country he had vacated. He wheeled in at the hitch rack in front of Keno Charlie's saloon and slid off, leaning his weight well into the horse.

He was a young man, normally smooth shaven, but now an inch of corn-colored stubble layered his cheeks. They made a pair, the horse and rider. Both were thin to the point of being gaunt, badly in need of a currying and clipping. The man's split-kneed jeans were supported by a frayed piece of lariat, but he hitched them up with a certain dignity, ducked under the hitching bar, and pushed through the batwings.

Keno Charlie's was nearly empty at this early morning hour, the sun not standing high enough to drive the November chill from the air. Three men stood at the bar, twirling their glasses, saying little, but they turned and gave him a frank glance when he came in. One of the men, much older than the other two, continued his inspection as if turning some thought over in his mind.

The free lunch table sat against the far wall, cluttered with stale sandwiches left over from the preceding night. This caught the stranger's eye, and he looked them over with the air of a fastidious gourmet. The three men turned to watch him. Even Keno Charlie paused in his glass polishing to give the young man his undivided attention.

A selection was made—a thick rye bread creation with drooping salami—and the young man bit into it. His chewing was a loud grinding sound in the silence. He finished the sandwich and attacked another, then went on to a third. The older man with the sharp blue eyes and blond hair that grew thickly at the temples and was turning white watched this with a faint amusement around the edges of his mouth. Keno Charlie said nothing until the fourth sandwich vanished, then threw down his towel. "Those are for the customers, mister!"

The young man paused in his meal, gave Charlie a frank stare, and said: "And I thank you. Someday I hope to be a customer of yours." He had one of those bland, open faces, and, although his pale eyes were bright with good humor, there was nothing brazen or bold in them.

"Don't take that free lunch too literally," Keno Charlie said with a forced gruffness, not knowing whether to turn sour or dismiss the whole thing.

"Let him alone, Charlie." The older man spoke softly. "You'd have thrown it out anyway . . . or else tried to feed it to Willie or Burt here."

"Dammit, John," Charlie murmured, "I can't afford to feed every saddle tramp that rides through."

The young man laid down his half-eaten sandwich, his fifth, and came over to the bar. He went through his pockets, finally coming up with a silver dollar that he laid on the bar. "In order to remove the stigma of vagrancy from my name," he said, "I will buy a beer . . . a large one with a very small head."

John Saber laughed at this. Charlie growled something under his breath, and the tap fizzled. Saber put his hand over the boy's dollar and shoved it back to him. "On me," he said. "You earned it with an all night ride."

The young man considered this for a moment, his face grave, then pocketed his dollar. He lifted his beer, and drank deeply, then wiped the foam from his lips with a tattered sleeve. He said to John Saber: "I thank you for the beer. Maybe we'll have another round when I'm more solvent. My name's Phil Stalker. I didn't catch yours."

Saber introduced himself and Willie and Burt Kerry, then they bellied against the bar and finished their beers.

Willie Kerry was a tall man in his early thirties with a wide, tolerant mouth and no nonsense in him. His eyes were grave, his actions studied and deliberate, and he wore a gutta-percha butted .44 with the bottom of the holster tied against his thigh. "What's your plans?" he asked Phil Stalker. "Winter's just over the next hill, and it's a hell of a time for seein' the country."

"I don't know," Stalker admitted. Then he asked: "What town is this?"

Keno Charlie's head came up quickly, his mind keening for the joke, but Phil Stalker's face was without guile. "Hondo," the saloonkeeper said. "You know you're in Texas, don't you?"

"Nope," Stalker admitted. "I been riding for two months, and the last place I recognized was Guthrie. Right now, I'm looking for a job."

"Doin' what?" Burt Kerry asked. He was a short man,

stocky, with heavy shoulders and a young, flat face. "You ain't a Westerner . . . a blind idiot can see that. This country ain't exactly for dudes."

Phil Stalker's eyes darkened for a moment, and he gave Burt Kerry a straight-faced attention. "You're right," he admitted. "I am an Easterner, but whatever I do, or say I'll do, will get no complaints from you or any man. I'm studying to be a lawyer, but I ran out of money at the end of this term, and now I'm trying to earn some to go back to school on. Is that all right with you?"

Burt looked from his brother to Saber, and then to Keno Charlie. He shrugged and said: "Hell, I just asked."

"I think," Saber said seriously, "that I just might have a job for you. A little monotonous and lonely maybe. Might even be a little risky in spots, but if you want it, it's worth sixty a month and found."

Willie Kerry became all caution. "Wait a minute, John . . . I don't know about this. We had two men before and didn't. . . ."

"All right," Saber said. "Can you leave your place and do it for me?"

Willie shook his head.

Saber turned to Burt Kerry and asked: "You're Cardigan's foreman . . . you got a man he can spare?"

"There's no arguin' with you," Burt said, and shoved his beer glass toward Keno Charlie for a refill.

"What kind of a job is this?" Phil wanted to know.

Saber took him by the arm, and the four of them crossed to a corner table and sat down. Saber scraped sawdust with his boot until he had a pile, then formed it into rough hummocks to model the surrounding country. He marked the roads with his fingertip, indicating the boundaries by a series of spaced finger marks. "We've been rustled for years," Saber explained. "We've cleaned out three bunches over a period of years, but some other bunch just moves in. Now here's my place. It runs from a mile south of the high road clear to the breaks that let down onto the flatlands. This is Wes Cardigan's Sunrise spread." He pointed to a scooped-out place depicting a large upper valley. "Down near the desert's edge is Jesse Dulane, Willie's father-in-law. Old man Rynder and Jim Hawk's place is over here . . . to the east a bit. Willie's got a place above me in the breaks, but the main trouble is a little farther on, just before the land lowers into the flatlands." He raised his head and called: "Hey, Charlie . . . bring us another round of beers, will you?

"Now," he went on, "I'm not trying to sell you a pig in a poke. Go into this thing with your eyes open and keep them that way. I have a cabin up in the breaks, and I'll set you up there above Willie's place. They've kept that country busier than the old Goodnight Trail, moving stock through. Now we've a good railroad here and loading pens, but there's one outfit that drives their cattle. They cut across the tip of my place and go out the south end through the cañon. I'm not asking you to fight my wars for me. Just look and remember what you see. We have the rope, and we'll use it when the time comes."

"I'm stone broke," Phil Stalker said. "I'll take the job, but I'll need a little stake." He took his brush jacket between his thumb and forefinger and held the thin cloth away from his body.

Keno Charlie arrived with four schooners of beer balanced on a tin tray, and Saber waited until he went back behind the bar before touching Burt Kerry on the arm.

"Take him over to Rutherford's store and see that he gets outfitted. Put it on my account."

"Hell!" Burt protested. "I just got my beer!"

John Saber sighed as if he were long accustomed to this, and Burt scraped back his chair, then stopped, half raised out of it.

The saloon door had opened, and a large, heavy-browed man entered. Two men followed closely behind. Willie Kerry and Saber turned to give them a heavy, friendless stare, and John's foot hastily erased his sawdust drawing.

Sam Bray leaned against the bar, his men strung out behind him, and said: "Gettin' cold out. Be snow in another week."

"We're ready for it," Saber told him.

Bray's dark brows knotted as he dropped his eyes to the pile of disarranged sawdust. He gave Phil Stalker a quick, searching glance, and his eyes narrowed. A sudden interest rose in his beefy, lined face. He turned and bellied against the bar.

Saber nudged Burt Kerry again and said quietly: "Get on with what I told you."

Kerry and Stalker went out together.

Rutherford's store was three doors down the street, and they entered it, navigating through a maze of hanging harness and stacked dry goods to come up against the counter. Phil Stalker made his clothing purchases and went into Rutherford's back room to change. He selected a heavy coat and a pair of sheepskin chaps, then gave his attention to the firearm counter. He examined a dozen handguns before taking a worn single-action Remington in .44 caliber. He scorned the hip holster, taking instead a skimpy holster that he placed under his left armpit.

Burt Kerry watched this with some amusement. "Saber will love you for that. He swears by them danged things."

"Some men swear *at* them," Phil said. He took a used Winchester from the wall rack. "It wouldn't make much difference where I wore a gun," he added. "I ain't fast, and with winter clothes on it'll be a lot easier to carry in a shoulder rig." He signed the chit, and told Rutherford: "I'll be back after this stuff later."

"No hurry," Rutherford stated. "It'll get paid for just the same."

Saber and Willie Kerry were waiting on the saloon porch. Phil halted before them, still cradling his rifle. Saber gave him a close, critical inspection, his eyes pausing on the bulge under Phil's left arm. He said: "Willie will get you a horse from Harris. He'll show you where the cabin is on his way home. If anything comes up . . . contact him. He'll get the word to me."

Stalker nodded, and walked with Willie to the end of Comanche Street. Harris's Livery Stable sat back from the road, and Kerry went in, coming out in a few minutes with a compact bay.

"What about my horse?" Phil wanted to know.

Willie grinned. "John will take it with him. The poor critter looks like he could stand six months of winter feed."

Bob Harris came from the restaurant across the street, a small, peppery man, and took his seat by the stable's arch. He watched Phil saddle the bay and said: "Stealin' one of my horses, Willie?"

Kerry winked at Phil. "You don't call that pigeon-breasted nag a horse, do you?"

Harris rose to his fighting best and waved a finger under Willie's nose. "I'll have you know," he shouted, "that that animal came outta Dixie Sweetheart who beat Harry Buck's chestnut four years ago!"

"Better talk a little louder," Willie remarked. "I don't think they can hear you down by the depot."

121

Harris sputtered. Phil swung into the saddle. Willie gathered his reins, and mounted.

"Who's gonna pay for the use of that horse?" Harris wanted to know.

"Saber," Willie said, and added: "You're gettin' pretty sassy lately, Harris. You better quit talkin' that way to me, or I'll stop givin' you my old razor blades."

They swung back up the street then, stopping before Rutherford's store while Phil made up a roll and started lashing it behind the saddle.

Sam Bray had come from the saloon with his two men, and they teetered on the edge of the boardwalk, watching Stalker.

"We got company," Willie murmured, and nodded his head, swinging Phil's attention around.

"They supposed to be somebody?"

Willie shrugged. "You could say they was in the cattle business, only we ain't proved it yet."

Stalker gave the men a bold-faced study. "They don't look so tough to me."

Willie grinned, and pulled at the lobe of his ear. "You know," he drawled, "I was just like you once . . . mule-headed and smart, too. Why, I knew it all. When I was eighteen, I thought my ol' man was the stoopidest person in the state of Texas. But when I got to be twenty-one, I was amazed at what he'd learned in three years."

Stalker gave him a quick grin and mounted. "Let's go," he said.

They rode out.

Hondo lay in a scooped-out bowl with high hills bracketing it on three sides, the higher mountains rising majestically beyond. High on the road, the desert seemed small and barren, lying off in the distance. Willie halted to rest the horses. He fashioned a smoke, his long fingers working over the paper until it was formed, then handed the tobacco sack to Phil Stalker. Although the sun stood high, a nail-sharp chill hung in the air, and Willie unrolled his heavy coat and slipped into it. He removed his gun belt, rebuckling it over the coat.

Stalker watched this and remarked: "You're a cautious man."

"I got a wife, and a daughter not a year old," Willie said. "I aim to live long enough to see her cut her first tooth."

Stalker swung his eyes over the country. The road wound before him, switching back and forth against the mountains, driving higher into the land beyond. "Wild country," he said.

Willie nodded in agreement. "Wes Cardigan's got the plum . . . a rich, high valley that runs for miles. Saber owns the most land but a lot of it is badlands. I got nine hundred acres of my own up in the breaks." He waved a hand to the right where the hills fell away to the desert's edge. "Sam Bray owns that. Not enough water on it to fill a bird bath, but he's built himself a nice herd."

Stalker asked: "You think he's night riding?"

"Never been able to prove it," Willie admitted. "We cut his herd now and then, but never found a thing. It's got us puzzled."

"Who around here's losing stock?"

Willie shrugged. "Everyone except Cardigan. Park Rynder's Pipe, Dulane's Anchor, the Leaning Seven . . . they all claim to have lost."

Stalker drew on his cigarette, then spun it away from him, and mounted. He said: "Looks bad for Cardigan, don't it?"

Temper and a proud stubbornness washed into Willie's face, but he clamped his lips together and swung up. He meant to move out, but the thing on his mind prodded him to speak. "Stalker, Cardigan's Sunrise wouldn't steal a blade of grass from no man. All of us owe Wes Cardigan something. Don't ever voice an opinion like that again."

"Sure," Phil said evenly. "I'm new here, and I just said what I thought. I meant nothing personal by it, and I didn't accuse your friend. However, if I actually suspected him, neither you nor the whole country could keep me from speaking my piece. You understand that?"

Willie stared at him for a long moment and Stalker's eyes never wavered. He was, Willie decided, a man ready to shake hands or fight on the slightest pretense. Somehow this pleased him, for he said—"We'll get along."—and rapped the horse into movement.

Talk seemed to come easier for both of them after that. It was as if they had reached out and felt each other's muscle and seemed satisfied with what they found.

Willie halted, and pointed to a large rabbit sitting thirty feet away. Phil shifted his rifle, but Willie shook his head, and drew his long-barreled .44. The shot split the stillness. The rabbit flopped twice, then lay still.

"Be good for supper," Willie said, and dismounted to retrieve the small animal.

The road at this point ran between sweeping grades, flattening to a small plateau. Willie picked the rabbit up by the ears, grinning, and skirted the larger rocks.

A clear voice said: "You ought to be more careful with your shooting."

Stalker swung his head at the sound. Willie pulled his gun with a speed that startled Phil. The rider sat above them, a rifle across the saddle, a small figure bundled tightly in a dirty sheepskin coat.

Willie shoved his gun back into the holster and said half crossly: "Come on down outta there, Anna. You ought to know better than to scare a man like that."

Phil looked again and saw that it was a girl. She lifted the reins, disappearing for moments at a time behind the boulders, then came out on the road and stopped six feet from them. Willie mounted and handed the rabbit to Phil.

Anna Bray said: "Who're you? I never seen you around here before."

Willie introduced him.

Anna said: "Oh. Another one." She was a pretty girl with large eyes, and a full, sad mouth. She watched Phil Stalker with a half-wistful expression and asked: "What do you want to go up there and live for?"

"Why . . . I . . . ," Stalker began.

Willie slid his voice in, cutting him off. "What's the matter, Anna? Having trouble at home?"

"I always have trouble," she replied, and glanced over her shoulder as if she expected to be followed. She lifted the reins. "It's been nice seeing you again, Willie . . . you, too, mister."

"Wait!" Willie said. He moved his horse closer to hers. "Anna, I don't mean to butt in, but if things get bad, you can always come to us or Saber."

"I'm all right," the girl insisted. "It's just that sometimes I get lonesome, that's all." She gave Phil a wan smile, then her eyes clouded with some thought. "You ought to leave the country, mister."

"What's the matter, Anna?" Willie asked.

A fear crossed Anna's face, and she said quickly: "Nothing, nothing. Good bye, Willie . . . good bye, mister."

She wheeled the horse, and shortly the sound of running hoof beats faded into nothing.

Willie sat, his hands folded on the saddle horn, puzzlement on his face.

Phil said: "She certainly is strange. She talks like she don't have good sense."

"She's got good sense," Willie assured him. "She's just scared of her own shadow, that's all. Her old man beats the skin off her every chance he gets, and don't ask me what for, 'cause I don't know." Willie let out a long, ragged breath. "We're just killin' time here."

They moved off, following the road as it bore deeper and higher into the land.

II

They raised Cardigan's ranch after three hours of riding. Willie took the horses into the barn while Phil loitered by the well. Wes Cardigan came out of the house and stood on the front porch, a big man, nearly fifty, with roan hair and a full mustache. Willie introduced Phil Stalker.

Wes Cardigan said: "Seems like you can smell my wife's cooking for ten miles, Willie."

They washed at the kitchen sink and seated themselves at the big, oval table. Lila Cardigan moved around the kitchen. Phil thought that she was a singularly beautiful woman with a full figure and pale blonde hair. She gave Stalker a guarded attention, then seemed satisfied at what she read, laughed, and entered into the small talk.

With the meal ended, Wes shoved his plate back and lighted a cigar. He fingered his mustache. "Snow in a few days. I can feel it in the air."

"A man gets all kinds of aches and pains when he gets old and stove up," Willie said, and pulled his face into a smooth mask.

Cardigan looked at him for a moment, then glanced at his

wife, and, when she laughed, his face broke, and he chuckled. "Damn' young Indian. Got a wife and a young 'un and still you run all over the country."

"Business," Willie Kerry told him, and reached for the coffee pot.

Cardigan shook his head sadly, positive the world was coming to a bad end and opined: "Why the devil you people can't live in peace is beyond me. All the time pickin' the other fella apart. You get a few head of cattle lifted and you start peekin' in your neighbor's window to see if he's tannin' the hide. There's always been a certain amount of sundownin' . . . there always will be. It's like sweat. You wash it off, and it comes right back."

Phil Stalker sifted tobacco into a brown paper. "They say that Sunrise beef hasn't been touched." He wiped a match alight in the dead silence, then lifted his eyes slowly and locked them with Wes Cardigan's.

Cardigan waited a moment, then said softly: "A statement like that could get a man in trouble."

The young man flipped the spent match into his saucer. "Whether it does or not remains to be seen. However, it was just a statement, not an accusation. I didn't make it up . . . just repeated it to you."

Cardigan's face lost some of its hostility, and he relaxed. "That's right, you didn't make it up, but you can't blame a man for bein' touchy." He let out a long breath. "No, I haven't lost a blasted head, and it's got me worried. Dammit, with all of my friends bein' rustled I feel slighted when I get left out."

Willie slapped his leg and stood up. "Time to be movin' on," he said, and went into the hall to get his coat.

They trooped outside, and Wes Cardigan went with them. He blew out his breath, watching it appear frosty in the biting air. "Come back in a few days, Willie. My three boys'll be home from that military school, and they'll want to see you."

"I'll do that," Willie said.

They swung up and rode out of the yard. An hour's easy ride carried them to Cardigan's fence, and they cut into the higher land, angling always toward the badlands. There was little talk between them. Stalker kept swinging his head from side to side, cataloging the terrain in his mind for future reference.

They cut through a high pass, and Willie stopped, pointing to a low cabin and outbuilding less than a mile away. "My place," he said with considerable pride. He pointed to a split in the distant hills. "Follow that and it breaks out on a small, high valley. Right over the rim the land cuts into a deep cañon that leads out onto the flatland. That's where Saber's cabin is. There's plenty of supplies there."

Stalker followed the pointing arm and nodded. He said: "Is that where they're driving them through?"

"Yep," Willie said. "Bray sure don't ship out of the railhead in Hondo."

"I wonder why?"

"You find that out," Willie told him, "and you can consider that you've earned your money."

"Anna Bray said something about me being another one. What did she mean by that?"

"John hired a couple of men before you," Willie said.

"What happened to them?"

Willie shrugged. "Got too tough for one, 'cause he quit. The other one we ain't found yet . . . but his horse came back."

Phil Stalker scratched the back of his head. "A cheerful thought."

"So long," Willie said. "Don't get caught asleep." He

grinned to ease some of the seriousness from his words. He cut down into the valley, disappearing a few minutes later among the rocks.

Stalker rode slowly through the land, and two hours later sighted the cabin near the end of a small valley. The sun was low in the sky; long shadows fell among the rocks. To the left of the cabin and down into a narrow cañon, the land split, forming a sheer wall that led to the flatlands miles beyond. He envisioned the land shaped as a gigantic bottle with the higher peaks marking the outline. He was the stopper. The thought gave him little comfort.

There were the hundred small things a man has to do when he moves into new quarters, and he spent the next two days rearranging things to suit himself. He cleaned out the nest of whisky bottles from under the bunk, and scrubbed the accumulated grime from the floor. Finally he removed the art decorations that cluttered up the walls.

True to Wes Cardigan's prediction, snow fell on the third day, at first only a thin blanket with gray skies that blotted out the half-warm sun. Toward evening of the third day it came down thicker, and soon a six-inch layer rounded the contours of the land, bringing with it a silence more muffled, more shrouded than he had ever known.

After the evening meal, he stretched out on his bunk, filled with the thoughts that solitude spawns. Sounds drifted to him, gently at first, then he sat upright as he caught the lowing of cattle in the cañon. He had no light burning, so he rose in the darkness and dressed. A few minutes later he went to the lean-to barn after his horse, the heavy Winchester cradled in his arm.

The snow stopped as he worked his way to the lower levels leading out of the cañon, and he had little trouble picking up the broad trail, even in the faint night light. Two hours of slow traveling brought him out of the hills and onto the flatlands where he could no longer track because the hard ground held no snow.

He was no Westerner, but he was not a fool, either, and he soon had a fair count of the herd. He had little difficulty separating the pony tracks and knew that he faced four riders should he overtake them. Their fire made a bright spot in the distance, not more than a mile away. He rode straight for it at a trot. He halted at their picket line about twenty yards from the fire and dismounted, cradling his Winchester in the crook of his arm. Sam Bray stood up, a great bear in his long fur coat. The three men with him remained seated, but alert.

Phil entered the ring of light and looked from one to the other, letting his eyes linger longest on Anna Bray who sat hunched against the cold, nursing a cup of coffee.

"You're a little out of your pasture, ain'tcha?" Sam asked. He glanced at the two men hunkered down near the fire.

"That's a fact," Phil admitted. "But it is such a fine point that I knew you wouldn't argue about it. Since the herd you pushed through tonight passed through Leaning Seven range, I thought I'd take advantage of the boss' rights and cut it, in case any of our steers got lonesome and joined up with yours."

"You got gall," one of the men said.

"Be good, Finley," Sam cautioned. "This young sprout is within his rights." He grinned at Phil, and jerked a thumb at the scowling man. "That's Finley Henshaw, my foreman. He's a little proud and touchy . . . you gotta forgive him." Bray's voice was heavy with friendliness. "You just go right ahead and look all you want to, sonny. They're all my cattle, registered to me, and I ain't got a thing to be afraid for you to see. Anna!" he shouted. "Go get a lantern for mister what's-his-name here to see with. You! Herman! Go with this sprout and see that he don't get lost."

The thin cowpuncher rose, and threw his plate on the ground, grumbling something under his breath, but he took the lighted lantern Anna handed to him.

Sam Bray's eyes glowed as if from some inner joke while Phil walked around the fire to join Herman. Anna Bray buttoned her sheepskin coat. Sam's rough voice sailed out: "Where the hell you goin'?"

She moved her head slowly until she looked over her shoulder at the scowling man. "With them," she said tonelessly. "I can use the fresh air."

Phil saw the urge to refuse vault into Sam Bray's face, but something held him, and he turned, showing them his back. They moved off into the night with only the bobbing lantern sending a puddle of light ahead.

He worked until midnight, going through the small herd slowly. They were all shorthorns and gave him no trouble. He examined each hip, reading the brands, Herman at his elbow holding the lantern and Anna making a shadow shape behind him.

Phil indicated that he was through, and Herman asked sarcastically: "You satisfied?"

"Yes," Phil admitted. "But there seems to be a great deal of irregularity in your branding. On some of the steers, the Cloverleaf brand is small . . . not more than four inches across, while on other steers it is eight and sometimes ten inches. How do you account for that?"

"You'll have to ask the boss," Herman said. He walked back to the fire ahead of Phil and Anna. The girl shot Phil a troubled glance, but he appeared to ignore her and followed the stringy cowpuncher.

Finley Henshaw had rolled up in his blankets, but Sam Bray still sat before the fire nursing his pipe. His hairy face was unreadable as he looked from his daughter to Stalker. "Everything suit you?"

Phil nodded.

Bray grunted: "I thought it would."

"There is something, though." Phil's voice was innocent. "I worked for a cattle outfit up in Wyoming last year, and they're very careful about their branding in that part of the country . . . but apparently you're not. I noticed all sizes. In fact, some of the artistry is very crude."

Sam's face settled, and he said with deceptive softness: "When a man uses the word 'artistry,' he's talkin' about a runnin' iron. Some men could twist that into bein' called a rustler."

Phil glanced over his left shoulder and found Herman studying him with a naked wariness. Anna's dark eyes showed a sudden alarm and that made up his mind for him. He shifted his body until the muzzle of the Winchester was pointed at Herman's breastbone and said: "Stand over here where I can keep an eye on you."

The man hesitated a moment. Phil worked the lever with a practiced speed. Herman got to his feet and stood by Sam. Bray placed his hands evenly on his knees. "You're just askin' for trouble, sprout."

"No trouble," Phil assured him. "Just a friendly call." He nodded to Anna and said: "Please bring me my horse."

The old man's eyes turned brittle, and he said quickly: "Anna, you stay still. You don't wait on nobody unless I say so."

"You'd better say so, then," Phil advised. He watched Bray and Herman. Henshaw still slept on; he made no move. Phil glanced at him—then took two steps toward him and jerked the blanket away.

The move took Henshaw completely by surprise. He tried to lift the gun he held cocked in his left hand, but Stalker swung the heavy barrel of his rifle in a downward arc, leveling the man without losing his advantage over the other two. Henshaw fell back, a long gash across his forehead. The blood ran off of his face onto the ground.

Sam Bray looked at the man without sympathy, then turned his angry eyes back to Phil Stalker. He said: "You can be rough on a man for nothin'."

"Depends on what you call nothin'." There was no give in the young man's face, and Sam nodded to his daughter.

The girl moved away, returning a moment later with his horse. Phil swung up, still covering them and backed out of the firelight.

He raised Willie Kerry's small ranch house just as a faint sun peeked over the rim of the land. Wood smoke spiraled up sluggishly in the still air, and the feeling of snow was stronger. He hailed the cabin, and dismounted by the log pole barn as Willie stepped out of the door, a wide smile across his blunt face. "If it ain't the young man of the mountain," he said. "Come on in. My wife's just settin' the table, and you look like a man that's tired of his own cooking."

A night without sleep had left Stalker a little frayed around the edges, and he followed Willie inside without comment. Louise Kerry was an uncommonly pretty girl with long brown hair done up in a bun. The baby sat at the table in a home-made high chair, gleefully flinging mush around the table and yelling happily at the top of her lungs. Louise smiled at Stalker and hastened to quiet her daughter. When some semblance of order was restored, they sat down to a meal of wheat cakes, long slices of bacon, and a platter full of fried eggs.

Willie stuffed his mouth full, chewed rapidly, and remarked: "I notice blood on your rifle barrel. You club a skunk?"

Phil said quickly—"In a manner of speaking . . ."—and told him of his nocturnal adventure.

Willie listened to this with a growing respect, while Louise shot him amused glances. "This pleases Willie, Phil. He and Henshaw have been blood enemies for over a year now. The man caught me swimming in the spring above our place and made a nuisance of himself. Willie got his gun and went hunting for Mister Henshaw. Fortunately John Saber and Jim Hawk intervened in town and cooled his hot head off before they could meet up."

Stalker glanced at Willie, then said: "After seeing him pull his gun, I'm not inclined to think of Henshaw sympathetically." He added: "We can just put the bump on the head down as part payment for the breakfast." He pushed back his plate, and reached for the coffee cup. "Anyway, Willie, we ought to tell Saber about this . . . the other ranchers, too. I have a few opinions about branding I'd like to air."

"All right," Willie agreed. "Give me the day to get them all together. You can come over here around sundown tomorrow night, and we'll go in together."

"Fine," Phil agreed, and got up from the table. He thanked Louise again for the meal and praised her cooking. He took the baby and held her aloft, much to her delight.

Louise was surprised. "She don't cotton to strangers as a rule. She's like my husband. If he likes you, then he'll do anything for you. If he dislikes you . . . well, he'd just as soon punch you in the nose as look at you."

Willie snorted at this, and went to the barn to saddle his horse. Phil placed the baby back in her high chair. "I can't figure that Bray girl out. When I was cutting that herd last night, she went along, but she didn't say anything . . . just stood behind me all of the time like a shadow. It gave me the willies, I can tell you that." He shook himself away from the thought and moved toward the door. "I'll be getting along, and thanks again for the meal."

He joined Willie in the barn and saddled up without a word of conversation. There was something in the young man's manner that didn't need talk to bolster it. He knew where he was going, and his movements were short and positive. He swung up and said—"See you tomorrow night."— and rode from the yard, angling toward his cabin high on the rim.

He spent the rest of the next morning riding and looking and the afternoon in a dreamless sleep. He woke when the sun was low against the edge of the land, heated a pan of water for his shave, and idled away fifteen minutes debating whether to sport a mustache like Saber or not. He studied his upper lip from several angles, then removed the hair with many practiced strokes.

The weather had turned nippy, and the air still carried the promise of snow, so he rolled his heavy coat and fur chaps to tie behind the saddle. He hid the rifle in the rafters, taking only his short-barreled Remington in the spring shoulder holster.

The horse bucked when he first mounted, and he put up with it for a half a dozen long-legged hops, then reined her into obedience and turned toward Willie Kerry's ranch. The sun was fully down and only a faint grayness layered the world when he came into Kerry's yard. The buckboard was before the door, hitched and ready to go. Stalker, after putting his horse in the lean-to, climbed onto the buckboard. Kerry and his wife had come out, and Kerry held the baby while she mounted. Then the three passed greetings back and forth, before settling down for the long ride to Leaning Seven.

There were four buckboards and one surrey at John Saber's front porch. The lamps on the bottom floor shafted light onto the snow-covered yard, and talk and laughter sailed out as they turned into the yard. Willie and his wife went into the house. Phil turned to the barn with the team and, after putting the horses in stalls, returned to the house.

He spent fifteen minutes shaking hands and meeting people he had never seen before, but who seemed to know him. Park Rynder leaned against a far wall, old and wrinkle-faced. Jim Hawk, his son-in-law, talked with him, a tall man with a grave mouth and eyes. Cardigan and his blonde wife were there. Saber's wife came in with a large tray of cookies and spoke softly to Louise Kerry. She was a small woman with shy eyes.

Jesse Dulane collared his son-in-law in the corner, and Willie laughed at one of the old man's rough jokes. Dulane was short with eyes that drew into slits when he laughed. Phil met Jim Hawk's wife, Mala, a tall, willowy girl with red hair and serious gray eyes. It was a pleasant room filled with pleasant people, he decided as he listened to the babble of the voices, soaking up the warmth of their friendship.

John Saber decided that they had had enough and pounded on the table for order. The talking died out. The women grouped together along the far wall, and the men became all business.

"Folks," Saber said seriously, "you know what luck I had with the last two men I hired to cruise the breaks for me. I'll tell you all now that I expected the worst when I hired this young man, but I'm wrong, and I want you to hear me say it. The saying that you can't tell the horse by the bridle certainly applies in this case. Willie told you all what happened, how

Phil buffaloed Henshaw. That proves something about the man to me. The boy thinks he's found something of value to us, and, by golly, if ever anyone deserved a listen . . . he does."

Saber sat down suddenly, and Phil Stalker was shoved out on his own. He took a piece of paper from his coat pocket and said: "No one has to tell you that you're losing stock, but I don't believe any of you can tell me where they're going." Phil leaned forward, placing both of his hands on the table edge. "I think I have the answer, a brand changer. By chance, the selection of your individual brands has opened up a brand changer's paradise."

"By God!" Jesse Dulane said, and the talk went around the room in a low hum.

Phil held up his hand, and they quieted. "Men, there are two distinct breeds of cattle thieves . . . the rustler and the brand changer. The rustler will steal a dozen, or a whole herd, and drive the hell out of them until he's put distance between himself and the former owner. He's a one-shot artist and doesn't stay long in one section of the country. Usually some irate cattleman stretches his neck."

He wiped a hand across his mouth and went on. "The brand changer works a little different. He works a country with brands he can doctor, sifting a few head at a time, and then drives the whole bunch to a market many miles away, and in the end he makes a lot of money."

He took a pencil from his coat pocket and beckoned them into a loose half circle around him. He drew the Leaning Seven, the Anchor, and the Pipe. Then he drew the Cloverleaf, Bray's brand. Going over the others again, he added the lines that made a cloverleaf out of each of them.

Jesse Dulane swore in a high, thin voice. Cardigan's mouth turned severe. Old Park Rynder's eyes showed a sudden temper, and the younger men grew sober-faced.

There was a silence in the room as they digested this.

Cardigan said: "That's clever, Phil, but pretty thin. It leaves a lot of questions unanswered. I can see now why Sunrise beef hasn't been touched . . . it'd be too hard to blot my brand, but again, if he worked all those over with a running iron, then they wouldn't be uniform."

"That's what I'm driving at," Phil said. "They aren't uniform. I noticed that last night and got to thinking about it. That's why he drives them over the mountains at night, so no one can see the brands in the daylight. How long do you think he'd last running them up the loading chute at the Hondo siding with some of you fellas sitting on the top rail looking on?"

They chewed it over a minute, then Cardigan said: "It's the piece we been looking for, all right, but I dislike the thought of riding on a man."

Willie Kerry spoke up. "There's where your two men went, John. They cut the herd, just like Phil did, and, once they saw the blotched brands, Bray couldn't let them go. One he must have bought off. The other fella is layin' out there in the rock somewhere with a bullet in him."

Saber stood with his head down, studying it out. He was the leader. They awaited his decision. "It figures," he admitted. He turned to Phil and declared: "They had it all set up for you too, son . . . Henshaw laying in his blankets with a gun, pretending to be asleep. Probably the same way they worked it the last time. You made it because you smelled a rat and jerked that blanket off. I don't think you'd better go back up there."

They were unanimous in that opinion. They crowded around the table, all talking at once, until Jesse Dulane pounded for attention. "By God!" he shouted. "We'll ride on that varmint and burn him out!"

"You're an old fire-eater," Jim Hawk told him. "I had a posse after me once with nothin' on their minds but hemp justice, and I didn't like it. I'm for goin' to the sheriff with this."

It divided their opinion like the stroke of a knife. Some wanted immediate action; others wanted the sheriff to handle it. Phil Stalker waited and listened, gauging the seriousness of it, then rapped for order.

They stopped, and looked at him. He said: "I'm trying to be a lawyer, and the first point of law is justice. You won't give Sam Bray justice with a torch and a Winchester."

Jesse Dulane's eyes sparkled. "*You* do all right with a Winchester."

"That's so," Phil agreed. "But *I* was in trouble. We can't prove Bray killed that rider of John's. We can't actually prove in a court of law that he rustled your cattle. You men fought to bring peace to this country, and that means a fair trial. A man is innocent until he's proven guilty. That's the law, and law and order is the only way."

Cardigan said in a heavy voice: "I move we take this to the sheriff."

Dulane held out for an immediate hanging, but Rynder was swayed, partly from the memory of his son-in-law, but mostly because he was a just man. Saber stood solidly behind Stalker for an appeal to the law. Gradually dissension died, and a few minutes later Jesse Dulane grinned and allowed that the country was going to hell, but he'd go along because he didn't want to get lonesome.

It was a cue to the women, and they rose. Then they were all talking again, and it seemed to Phil Stalker that they had never mentioned rustling.

The buzz in the room grew, and he was pulled into the conversation. Over in the far corner there was hearty laughter, and Jesse Dulane's—"By God."—but Phil decided he liked the sound of it and wondered how he had ever lived for twenty years without these people.

III

Hondo's main street was slick with frost and rough with frozen ruts. Rooftops were glazed white and sparkled in the early morning sun as Phil Stalker and John Saber turned onto it and dismounted before the arch of Harris's Livery Stable. They cut diagonally across the street to the sheriff's office. Finding the front door unlocked, they entered. The room was chilly and raw, and Saber opened the door of the pot-bellied stove and kindled a fire. He fed it wood until it glowed, and a damp warmth flooded the room. Somewhere in the rear cell block a drunk wailed about "these prison walls" in an alcoholic tenor. Saber smiled, then straightened when Harms came from his room, pulling his suspenders over his fat shoulders.

"What's so important that a man will get out of a warm bed and ride fifteen miles?" Harms wanted to know.

"I want a warrant sworn out for Sam Bray," Saber said, getting immediately to the point.

"Well, now," Harms hedged. "I don't know. You got evidence against the man?"

Phil Stalker repeated his story, and Harms heard him through. He said: "Sonny, was I to arrest Bray, I wouldn't be able to hold him on that amount of evidence, let alone get a conviction. And if I turned him loose, then this country wouldn't be safe for you."

Saber's mouth flattened, and he rolled a smoke to collect his thoughts. "You won't make an arrest, then?"

"Dammit, John," Harms said testily, "you was a U.S. marshal for nine years. You know where a lawman stands and where he don't stand."

Saber recognized the truth of it. "Of course," he said. "Thanks anyway, Sheriff."

They went out and stood on the boardwalk, suddenly with nothing to do and no place to go.

Phil said: "I suppose it'll be the torch now?"

"You object?"

"Hell, yes, I object!" Stalker said. "Law is law. Cut one corner and then you'll cut another. Pretty soon it'll get bad enough to where they send a Texas Ranger in and clean it out." He shook his head. "We'll have to do it some other way. I'll go back up there and prowl around. Maybe I can turn up something."

"Maybe you can turn up dead, too," Saber said. "You better stay around the ranch house. We'll find some sort of a winter job for you."

Stalker shook his head. "You hired me for that line shack. If you don't want me up there any more, just say so, and I'll ride out and find some other job."

"Oh?" Saber said. "What about those clothes and stuff? You must be in to me for a hundred dollars anyway."

"Then I'll send you the money when I get it," Phil said. "I either finish the job I started, or you can go to the devil."

Saber stared at the boy for a moment, then began to chuckle.

"What the hell's so funny?"

"I was thinking of Willie Kerry," Saber replied. "You and him ought to have a lot of fun butting heads together. I don't rightly know which of you is the hardest, but it'll be interesting to find out."

"Let's go over to Keno Charlie's and have a drink," Phil

urged. Saber's face mirrored his puzzlement, and Phil added: "I told him once I was going to be a cash customer. Loan me five dollars."

"Think I'll ever get it back?"

Stalker took the gold piece and said—"That's a chance you take, friend."—and they walked across the street.

They had a beer apiece, and Phil ate three sandwiches, much to Charlie's disgust. Then they went to Harris's after their horses. The ride was a silent one, since neither of them was given to talk. They said a brief farewell at Saber's front porch, after which Phil cut across the land toward the higher country.

He made his evening meal, and went to the spring for a bucket of water. Snow began to fall in great flakes, almost straight down. There was no wind behind it. He lighted the lamp and ate, then heated water to wash the dishes. This chore done, he gathered the dishpan and crossed to the door. He opened it with his free hand.

A muffled figure was poised there.

Phil reacted instinctively. He threw the pan and dishwater in the man's face, and lashed out with a knotted fist, catching the surprised victim squarely on the shell of the chin.

He snatched his Remington from his shoulder holster, and cocked it. He said in a badly rattled voice: "Get up or I'll shoot!" But he had underestimated the power of his punch, for the man was completely out.

The solitary lamp gave out little light, the door remaining in deep shadows. Phil holstered his gun and dragged his victim into the cabin, toeing the door closed and sliding the bar. The figure's hat was tied low over the ears with a heavy scarf. Phil removed these with a savage yank. He gasped when Anna Bray's dark hair tumbled out onto the floor.

He struggled with her inert form, and finally got her placed on his bunk. He removed her coat and gloves, bathed her face until she stirred.

Anna opened her eyes, and it was a moment before they completely focused. "That was a terrible thing to do," she said.

"I'm very sorry," Phil said. "I really am."

"You should be," Anna told him, and he saw that she was not angry.

"What are you doing here?"

She lay back on his bunk, and he crossed to get the lamp from the table. She was a very pretty girl, he saw then. Her eyes were large and dark, and there was no guile there. This, he wondered about. Her hair was dark and wavy, and he liked that.

Anna said: "I know what you're trying to do to my father . . . only he isn't really my father. My mother married him after *my* father died."

"That still doesn't tell me what you're doing here," Phil said.

Anna took a deep breath and plunged into the thing. "I want to make a bargain with you. My safety and a new start for the thing you need to hang my step-father."

Phil frowned. He had a strong sense of justice, and this set none too well with him. "A poor way to do business . . . dealing off of the bottom of the deck that way."

She had pride. "You're a man," she said. "You can fight with your fists and a gun, but I'm a woman. I do the best I can and have no regrets. He's turned into a dog that's jealous of every man that has one acre more . . . one cow more than he has. I'm tired of being beaten and treated like a prisoner . . . never trusted, always watched. I want out, that's all."

"How do you mean . . . 'out'?"

"Money," she said. "Oh, not much. Just enough to tide me over until I can get a job in some other town. I can work. I'll manage once I get away from him."

Phil sighed because he saw how great was her need. "All right, you got a deal. I'll speak for Saber, and he'll back what I say. Is that good enough for you?"

She nodded. "Did Saber tell you about the other men he had up here?"

Phil nodded.

She went on. "One of them, Sam bought for three hundred dollars before he ever saw a blotted brand. The other one was like you . . . stubborn. He's buried under the compost pile back at Sam's ranch."

"How can you prove it's he?"

"His gear's there," Anna said. "Saber would recognize it." She waited until he turned it over in his mind, then asked: "Is that enough?"

"Yes," he said.

He rose and took her coat, holding it before the fire until it got warm. He held it for her while she put it on, then she asked: "Where am I going?"

"To Willie Kerry's place," Phil said. "Tell him I said to take you to Saber's. You'll be safe there."

She studied him levelly as she retied her scarf. Phil realized that she was interested in him as a man. She said: "You gave me an awful whack on the jaw."

He flushed and lowered his eyes. She opened the door and went out. He blew out the lamp and stood in the open doorway watching her. She made a dim shadow as she mounted and rode out of the yard.

He gathered up his fallen dishpan and hung it back on the wall, then closed the door, and dampened the fire for the night. He didn't undress, for some inner caution took hold of him, but stretched out on the bunk with his heavy Winchester by his hand.

He dozed and woke and dozed again, rising once to replenish the wood in the stove. He opened the door and peered outside and saw it was still snowing. A foot-thick layer now blanketed the ground. He thought he heard a curb chain, moved his head to one side like a dog to listen. He leaped back into the cabin and slammed the door as the night blossomed color and a bullet tore through the planking.

Sam Bray's deep voice boomed in the following quiet. "What do we gotta do . . . smoke you out?"

"Try it!" Phil called back. "You can only get killed so dead!"

Sam's voice was low and plain. "Shoot a couple more rounds through the door, Finley." There was a pause, and a shot ripped through the wood at an angle, imbedding itself in the far wall. Phil scooped up his Winchester and crossed to a small side window. They sat their horses not twenty feet away, and Finley Henshaw was feeding another shell into the breech of his trap-door Springfield. The snow made a sufficiently light background to silhouette Henshaw as he raised the rifle for another shot. Phil shoved the muzzle of his rifle through the glass, and, as Henshaw squeezed off, Phil fired at the bright muzzle flash. He saw Finley Henshaw leave the saddle as if mauled to the ground by a giant hand.

Sam swore and yelled: "Into the rocks . . . into the rocks, dammit!"

Phil heard the bullets *thud* into the stovepipe as they shot it off even with the roof. A moment later smoke began to back up in the flue, and, when it became thick and strong, he knew that they had him boxed in. He put on his heavy chaps and coat, then returned to the window and fired three rapid shots from his Remington, attracting a wicked volley in return. He dashed for the door and was out into the night, running in a low crouch. He counted on their being momentarily blinded by their own muzzle flash and was ten feet from Henshaw's horse when Sam bawled—"There he is, you damned fool!"—and snow flew in a cold shower.

Stalker didn't bother to return the fire, but vaulted into the saddle and stormed out of the yard. Sam's cursing followed him for a time, then was lost as he widened the breech. He paused ten minutes later to look back. There was a growing glow on the horizon. It filled him with a hard anger, and he tried to rationalize it, then gave it up and kneed the horse into motion.

Two hours later he came to Cardigan's fence and dismounted to let himself through. He followed it until he came to the fork in the Hondo road, then cut west into the flatter land and Bray's Cloverleaf range. Saber's ranch lay to the left and slightly behind, and he drove on, keeping the horse at a killing pace. He let the animal have its head, and it took him where he wanted to go—Sam Bray's barn.

There was no light in the cook shack or bunkhouse. This being Saturday night the hands would be in Hondo. That suited him. He found hay stacked in the rear of the barn and a lantern hanging from a stanchion. He shattered it with his gun barrel, letting the coal oil run over the loose hay. He found a match and soon had a roaring blaze going. Using a pitchfork, he carried burning hay to the bunkhouse and the cook shack, then turned the horses loose, driving them off with rapid blasts of his revolver.

The house came next. He started a fire in the kitchen, carrying it to the south bedroom, and was busy igniting the parlor when Sam Bray and Herman rode into the yard.

Bray was cursing in a crazy voice and running back and

forth, illuminated by the ghostly flickering. Stalker paused at one of the front windows, shattered it with his rifle butt, and flung a shot into the snow at Bray's feet.

Sam halted and raised his rifle, returning the fire, unmindful of the fact that he was outlined against the burning barn. Herman ran toward the bunkhouse, then changed his mind, and dashed back across the yard, yelling and shooting wildly. Phil took refuge in Bray's small office where the flames had not yet eaten.

Bray got control of himself and found cover behind the watering trough. Herman stationed himself behind the well curbing. Together they effectively pinned the young man down. Somewhere in the rear of the house—Phil assumed it was the kitchen—a great crashing rose as the fire-eaten timbers parted and let a wall fall away. The heat became intense, and the light spread to a great perimeter. Bray and Herman kept up their fire.

Phil held his fire, conserving his few remaining cartridges. He had but little time left—he reached that conclusion with no difficulty. The house was old and the wood dry, and he had done an excellent job of firing it. "Well," Phil said to himself, "here goes nothing." He gathered himself for the dash through a broken window. He gripped his rifle and rose—then paused.

Saber and the two Kerry boys were storming into the yard with Cardigan and Jim Hawk following closely behind.

Herman, always a little slow to catch on, tried to raise his gun. Someone shot him in the thigh, and he sat down with no fight left.

Sam Bray lost no time discarding his gun and stood with his hands shoulder high. Phil Stalker quickly left the burning house. Willie and Burt Kerry covered Herman, who lay in the snow and groaned. Cardigan and Jim Hawk secured Bray to a saddle horse with a length of lariat.

John Saber smiled when he saw Phil Stalker. He turned to Burt and said: "Ride into town and get the sheriff."

Burt's mouth dropped open, and he said: "Hell, I just got here!"

Saber smiled faintly. "You going to argue?"

Burt rode out.

Saber dismounted, and stamped his legs to speed up the circulation. He looked around him at the burning ruins and said to Stalker: "I thought you was long on law and order . . . innocent until proven guilty. I thought you was solid against this torch law."

Phil looked sheepish. "A man can get pushed just so far, and then there's an end to it."

Willie Kerry edged his horse closer to get in on the conversation. "See what bein' stubborn gets you?"

"You go to the devil," Stalker told him.

"I might if I hung around a heller like you," Willie said.

Phil turned serious and asked: "Is Anna all right?"

"Safe at my place," Saber said, then pursed his lips thoughtfully. "She heard the shooting and rode for Willie's like you told her to." He gave Phil a long glance and added: "You put my foot in it good when you made her that promise, sprout. You didn't have anything special in mind, now, did you?"

Stalker looked at Willie who was leaning over in the saddle, both arms crossed over the horn, a vast amusement plastered over his face. Phil switched his gaze to Saber and saw a smile around the usually severe mouth. "Dammit all," he said, "I ain't met her but three times. Aw, hell . . . she is a pretty thing, and I want to be a lawyer. I thought if she had a home and you knew me and you knew her, well . . . you know what I mean."

"I see," Saber said. He lowered his head to roll a cigarette, covering his expression with these small movements.

Phil glanced at Sam Bray who sat his horse with his head down, not looking at any of them. It was over, but somehow it wasn't finished in Phil's mind. He crossed over to the man and said: "You called me a sprout . . . well, that's what I am and you were right, but I'm old enough to know that whatever a man does, he does it for a reason."

"What you tryin' to do . . . ease yer conscience?"

"That's right," Phil admitted. "I've done a lot of things I never believed in before, and I'm trying to justify it. I never killed a man or even shot at one until tonight. I can live with that, but I'd like to know why a man like you thinks he has the right to mess up other people's lives."

Sam raised his head and looked at John Saber, then at Cardigan who stood in the background, talking to Jim Hawk. "Look at 'em," he said. "Bloated with land and cattle. They got the whole country to themselves . . . them and their friends. It just ain't right."

"I guess to you it isn't," Phil said, and turned away from the man.

Saber drew long on his smoke, then stepped on it. "So you're going to be a lawyer?" he said. "Takes humility in a man to look at another man and believe in him when everyone else is against him. Do you have that kind of humility, sprout?"

Phil Stalker looked over his shoulder at Sam Bray, sitting forlorn and beaten on the horse. Stalker thought about Saber's question, then nodded.

The tall blond man studied him in the flickering light of the burning buildings and said softly: "Damned if I don't believe you have at that."

149

The Sheriff's Lady

I

The first grayness of dusk had settled over the land and shop lights cross-barred the loose dust of Comanche Street as Willie Kerry turned into Bob Harris's Livery Stable at the south end of town. Buggies stood in a haphazard cluster around the darkened maw, and Kerry got down, lifting his wife to the ground. Harris came out, a withered man with a foul-smelling pipe clenched in his toothless jaws.

"Good night for business," Kerry said.

Harris's reply was only a soft grunt. He unhitched the team, leading them into the stable. Kerry looked up and down the street, then excused this moment of idleness by rolling a smoke. He was a lanky man with a deep gravity on his blunt face. Hair lay in dark chunks across his forehead, and his fingers were blunt with short, curling hairs on the back.

He took his wife's arm, and they walked toward the hotel a half block down the street. He glanced at her as they came into a path of light cascading from a shop window. Louise was a tall girl, full-breasted, with thick brown hair framing a face tanned by a lifetime in the sun. Her eyes were pale like his, and her full mouth curved at the ends, reflecting some inner gaiety that she habitually concealed. Willie glanced at the rigs dotting the half dark street and said softly: "Looks like Saber and the others mean business, don't it?"

She nodded. "Try not to lose your temper, Willie. Some of them are set in their ways."

They paused at the hotel steps. He removed his hat, when he faced her, and her eyes glowed at this courtesy. It was not a studied thing with Kerry, this gallantry; it stemmed from deep within him. It was as if he never had fully recovered from the miracle of this woman's love for him.

He said: "I saw Jim Hawk's buggy. I guess Mala and the other women are in the hotel. I'll try not to be too long."

She touched his hand. It was a fleeting gesture that caused a smile to break across the severity of his face. "You do what's right, Willie." She turned and entered the hotel. He watched her enter the lobby, then placed his hat squarely on his head, and crossed the street to Keno Charlie's saloon.

Mose Dinwitty handled the sparse trade at the bar. He nodded toward a back room when he saw Kerry. Willie entered without knocking.

John Saber raised his head at the interruption and broke off his talk. He gave Willie a friendly smile. "Where's Jesse Dulane?"

"Couldn't get away," Willie said. "He's watching our girl. I'll speak for him."

"Good enough," Saber said. He turned to the others crowding the small room. "I guess we're all here. Let's get it over with."

Wes Cardigan leaned against a far wall with two of his sons. He had a long, tolerant face, and a full, drooping mustache hid his mouth. He said: "Somehow I keep gettin' the feelin' that we oughta wait. Election's only three, four months off. Hell, it ain't that important."

151

Saber shot him a quick, irritated glance, and Cardigan fell silent. Saber looked at the others in turn, and it cut the hesitation and uncertainty like a quick sweep of a knife. John Saber had a long, hooked nose and eyes that bored into a man like drill steel. He wore a black suit with a string tie loose against his white shirt front. His blond hair was thick and white at the temples. He had a great dignity about him. He said: "All of you know that Harms has disappeared. Now he wasn't much of a sheriff, but he was the law we had. All along now, that desert bunch has got bolder and a little tougher. Dale Simpson got run out of Morgan Tanks a week ago, just before Harms went over there. The time has come to put a strong man in Harms's place and let him handle that bunch."

Jim Hawk shifted in his chair, heavy-faced, but careful with his speech. "Is appointin' a man this way legal, John?"

Saber rolled a smoke with infinite patience, answering only when he had completed the cylinder and touched a match to it. "Phil Stalker's a lawyer. He's representing the townsmen in this vote. He can give you an answer to that."

"It's legal," Stalker said, "until election. Then the ballot goes to the voters in the county, the desert bunch included."

"What about that desert bunch?" Park Rynder wanted to know. He was a short man, peppery in nature, who spoke in quick spurts. "Them people have been hollerin' for a split in the county for ten years. I say let 'em have the damn' desert and hash out their own troubles."

"That's no good," Cardigan said heavily. "They can't abide by the law as it is now. How can they govern themselves?"

"We gotta do somethin' about this," Dan Isbel stated. He was a slow-thinking man, always lagging behind in the conversation. He shifted his bulk uncomfortably as this outburst

152

drew eyes and covered his confusion with the small motions of lighting his cigar.

Saber said: "As usual, Dan has cut to the meat of the problem. We gotta do something now, not at election time."

"Let's get the hell at it," Bob Overmile said. He made a thin, high shape in the corner. Willie's brother, Burt, stood beside him, dark and blocky with a wide mouth and his own solitary thoughts.

John Saber sat down at the end of a long table. He allowed a thick silence to settle over the room, permitting it to stretch before breaking it. He had that natural showmanship, that perfect sense of timing that swung men's attention to him. He spoke at last, and, for some reason that none of them fully understood, it seemed a relief.

"We must face facts. Harms never got anywhere with that desert bunch. They're a proud lot, clannish, and they hate any outsiders. They whipped the water situation out there, and now that they're enjoying a mild prosperity, they seem to think that what our county officers say don't count."

"You still ain't said who you're gonna appoint," Jim Hawk reminded.

Saber glanced at Cardigan and Park Rynder. He said: "I think Willie Kerry's the man to go out there and ram a little law down their throats."

Kerry's head came up with startling suddenness. "Now wait a minute," he said. "I don't want the damn' job. Give it to Overmile . . . he's out of work."

"If the man don't want to go," Dan Isbel said, "he don't have to go."

"It ain't that I don't want to assume my obligation," Kerry stated. "But I got a family and a place of my own to take care of. Three months is a long time, especially right now when shippin' time's only a month off."

"I'll take care of your place for you," Overmile said briefly. "Be a good place for me to roost until the slack time's over." It seemed to settle the question, for they nodded and muttered among themselves.

Willie touched each of them with his eyes, then said to Saber: "Why me, John?"

Saber pulled at the ends of his mustache. "You got a good head, and you're tough, but I figure the head's more important right now than a killer instinct."

"What about Harms?" Isbel wanted to know. "You think the desert bunch killed him?"

Saber shrugged. "Hard to tell, Dan. He's been gone a week, and nobody's seen him. Some of the boys have been out for the last day or two, but we ain't turned up anything. We'll keep looking, though. A man don't just up and disappear in thin air."

"Do I gotta take this job?" Willie asked suddenly.

"No," Saber stated, but he drew the *no* out, placing a lot of *yes* in it. "Decide for yourself."

Willie thought of Louise, then, and said: "I'll let you know in an hour . . . all right?"

Saber nodded, and Willie left the room.

Keno Charlie called to him on the way out, and Kerry halted along the bar. "They decide what happened to Harms yet?"

"Still a mystery," Kerry said. He went out and across the street to the hotel. Louise sat in a far corner, talking to a small group of women. She saw Willie enter the lobby and excused herself.

She read the look on his face and said: "You, Willie?"

His eyebrows went up in surprise. "You knew about it?"

"No," she told him. "It was just a guess. You were the logical one."

He blew out his breath through tight lips. "Damned if I can figure that. Anyway, I told them that I'd let them know in an hour. I don't have to take it if I don't want it."

She took his arm, and they went outside, walking south on Comanche Street until they came to the first cross street. The courthouse square sat back from the road, and they cut across the grass, taking seats by an old Civil War cannon. Willie fashioned a cigarette, then a match flared, casting a small light over the uneven plains of his face.

Louise said: "I don't want you to hold back because of me, Willie."

"I don't like to leave our place," he said. "Morgan Tanks is a rough town. That whole part of the country is a hotbed of trouble. A man would never know when it'd blow up in his face."

"We wouldn't be there forever," Louise said.

"You're not just sayin' that to make me feel good?"

She smiled and leaned forward to kiss him. "Go back and tell them that you'll take it." He hesitated, and she urged him with a small pressure of her hands. "Grandpa can baby sit. He loves it. Go on now. I'll wait for you at the hotel."

She had that wisdom that often plumbed his innermost desires. He knew he would not want to live without it. "I won't be long," he said, and left her, disappearing a moment later down the darkened side street.

Saber and the others had laid a blue haze of cigar smoke in Keno Charlie's back room by the time Kerry returned. Willie stepped in, and closed the door. Talk ceased abruptly.

Saber said: "What about it, Willie?"

"I guess I'm the sheriff," Willie said. "If that's the way you fellas want it."

"That's the way we want it," Saber said, and stood up to

administer the oath of office. There were murmurs of approval when Saber pinned the six-pointed star to Willie Kerry's coat.

They filed out of the back room, and bellied against the bar. Keno Charlie and Mose Dinwitty both hastened to serve them. Kerry accepted a cigar and a drink, in that order, and turned his head as the front doors opened. A quiet settled over the saloon as their voices and soft laughter died in a rippling wave.

The man who stood there was not tall or impressive, yet every eye clung to him. He moved to the small ell at the end of the bar, and placed his hands evenly on the polished surface.

Park Rynder said: "I know this man. What do you want here, Randolph?"

"Talk," Randolph stated. "I left my gun outside . . . along with my fight. I just got a word for the new sheriff."

Willie studied the young man with considerable interest. He was roughly dressed, with a cowhide vest covering a faded gray shirt. His jeans were thin from repeated washing, and his boots were flat-heeled with square toes. The dark of his skin, along with the extremely wide-brimmed hat, marked him as a desert man. He had a wariness bred from the solitude and vastness of that wasteland.

Kerry nodded to Charlie. "Give Mister Randolph a drink, Keno."

Randolph's eyes swung to Kerry, and a tight pride went into his face. "I want nothin' from you . . . from any of you!"

Kerry leaned both elbows on the bar. "Thirty miles across the desert is a hot ride. The drink was a courtesy from one man to another. We may not like each other, but we ought not snap like dogs, either."

Saber's head came around quickly at this unexpected mildness. Kerry continued to watch Randolph and saw a

156

small mollification of that stubborn pride.

Randolph said in a low voice: "Thanks . . . I'll have that drink if you don't mind."

Willie took the bottle from Mose, and walked to the end of the bar. They drank together.

Randolph said: "I can see you're the new law. I got a message for you then . . . don't come onto the desert with that badge!"

Every man in the room held his breath, but Kerry surprised them with his reaction. His lips pulled thin, but no anger crept into his eyes. His voice was conversational. "I can see that you ain't the kind of a man who'd make threats . . . you're just statin' facts. I'll be in Morgan Tanks within a week to set up an office. That ain't a threat, either. It's a fact that I'm statin', too."

Randolph said: "I said what I was told to say. I got nothin' personal to add."

"I treat people just like they treat me," Willie told him. "I hope you remember that."

"I'll tell Kileen you said it," Randolph promised. He turned to leave, but Willie caught him by the sleeve.

"You know these men here?" Willie asked, and waved a hand at Cardigan and the others.

Randolph's forehead tightened into deep wrinkles. "No," he said, "and I don't want to, either."

"I knew a fella once," Willie stated, "who wouldn't take a drink of whisky because he was afraid he'd get to likin' it. A fella could be that way with men, too."

Randolph's face filled with a driving temper. "You tryin' to make a fool outta me?"

Kerry recognized a man on the edge of a fight. "Not at all. I just thought you'd like to know men who work like hell for a living, drink the same brand of whisky you do, and cuss the same things." He waited for a tight moment, then Saber walked over to them and offered Randolph another drink.

Some measure of relief crossed Kerry's face when Randolph accepted, and the others came forward. No one broke his back being friendly, but neither was there strain in the low talk and lifting of glasses. Randolph finished his drink, thanked them civilly, and went out. A moment later the sound of his running horse faded.

Park Rynder said: "If that don't beat anything I ever seen."

Keno Charlie rattled glasses as he set them up again on the house. A wide grin split his thin face. "I been passin' booze over this bar for eighteen years now, and that's the first time I ever seen a desert man drink with a man from the breaks."

The others laughed and joked about it, but John Saber's face remained long and thoughtful. He said to Kerry: "I expected you to belt him. What were you trying to prove, anyway?"

Willie was surprised. "John, I wasn't tryin' to prove anything. I guess I was thinkin' of this badge and some of the responsibility that goes with it. No man will obey the law if he don't respect it."

"Sometimes you puzzle me," Saber said, and finished his drink. He glanced at his watch. "Edith's waiting. I'd better get along." He gave Kerry another long glance. "Don't think too much about that star. And don't trust Kileen. He's a wild one. Folks out there sorta look up to him as a leader."

"The man gets his chance along with the rest of 'em," Kerry said, and Saber shrugged before walking out.

They broke up then, and Willie crossed the street to the hotel. His brother was sitting on the verandah with Louise. Burt said: "I'll move my stuff out there in the morning. Don't worry about a thing, Willie. Overmile and me'll handle it for you."

"Worryin's for the feeble-minded," Kerry stated. He took his wife's arm. They went inside and registered for a room.

II

Hondo lay on the desert's edge, buttressed on the south by hills that rose to form ragged backbones and deep valleys. The desert to the north remained to challenge all who looked upon it. For forty miles it stretched out, flat and simmering, under a brassy sun, baked white by the heat and driven into graceful hummocks by the wind. Only sage and cactus broke the monotony of its flatness, with the town of Morgan Tanks sitting near the northern fringe, squat and unpainted and bleached the color of sand.

Willie drove hunched over in the seat of the buckboard. His wife sat in silence beside him, trying not to acknowledge the heat that dampened her dress with sweat and the dust that coated her flesh. A trunk and three suitcases rode behind them, shifting slightly as they passed over a road that was little better than faint wagon tracks across the vastness.

Willie's hat rode low over his forehead as a shield against the sun. He said: "Men are sure funny critters. Who'd ever think they'd come here and ranch this sand."

It was too hot for talk. He hadn't expected her to answer him and was not surprised when she remained silent.

Morgan Tanks lay in a loose sprawl on the horizon, and they entered it an hour later. It consisted of a narrow main street and three back streets. Main was flanked by a saloon, two stores, a hotel, and several small merchants' establishments. Kerry pulled up before the hotel. Three men sat on the gallery, testing the shade, and they fastened a hard-eyed attention on him as he dismounted to lift his wife to the ground. He wore no coat. The badge was pinned to his white shirt front. He surveyed the town with a quick critical eye, then took Louise's arm and mounted the porch. He signed for a room, saw that she was settled and the baggage stowed, then returned to the verandah and the three men who waited in sweltering patience.

A tall, raw-boned man with a touch of white in his hair stood up.

Willie said: "I guess you're Kileen."

"You're Kerry then," Buck Kileen said in a deep, soft voice. "Didn't you get Randolph's message?" His eyes traveled Willie's length quickly. He saw that the sheriff carried no gun and asked curtly: "Are you trying to prove something without a gun?"

Willie shrugged. "Too hot to wear a harness," he said, and sat down on the porch railing. "I've heard a lot about you, and I'm impressed. It takes a great man to sink a well for six hundred feet and get water, then irrigate twenty square miles with it. A man'd think you'd have enough sense to obey the laws, or listen to reason, without tryin' to order a man around like you had Randolph do."

Kileen snorted. "I break none of your damn' laws. Harms shoved his weight around, and we don't like that out here. We're big enough and rich enough for our own county. We don't need Harms and his law."

"What happened to Harms?"

Kileen's eyes filled with stubbornness. "You just find that out for yourself."

"I intend to," Willie assured him. "In the meantime, I'd like to set up an office and jail here. I could use some cooperation from you."

Kileen rose, and his men with him. He tapped Kerry on the chest with a stiff finger. "Harms wanted to set up an office, too. You're only one man, and you'll leave with your tail tucked between your legs."

Willie watched with grave concern as Kileen stomped off of the porch. He sighed, and stepped into the street, the sun striking him with a fiery breath. He walked until he came to the empty building by the harness maker's.

He found the door unlocked and went in, brushing cobwebs with his hat. At some time in the past it had been a strong jail. Two small cells stood in the rear corners. He went out, coming back twenty minutes later with a carpenter and the blacksmith. By evening he had the place in good repair and a sign over the door proclaiming it to be a branch of the county jail.

He and his wife took their evening meal in the hotel dining room, ignoring the open stares and cutting glances.

Willie said: "I wonder what the devil's eatin' these folks? That fella, Kileen . . . he ain't a snarly man by nature, but he sure gets his hackles up when he sees a badge."

"There are women in this town," Louise said. "Tomorrow I'm going to find someone to talk to. Sometimes a woman can find out more than a man can."

Willie grinned. "Maybe I ought to make you a deppity." He turned his head when he heard a sheet of glass shatter. He put his fork aside, moving toward the front door.

The sun was not entirely dead, and enough light layered the land for him to see the street clearly. Randolph stood in the middle of the dust, facing a small bakery. Glass glittered on the boardwalk, and he hefted another rock as if searching for a larger target.

A young girl detached herself from the shadows across the street and came up to pull at his arm. He shook her off, speaking sharply, and she went back to the boardwalk. He saw Kerry and let his eyes rest on him for a daring moment, then turned and threw the rock through the window of the mercantile. He turned again and entered the saloon.

Willie glanced up and down the street. Nearly seventy-five people stood along the walls. He knew what this was, and there was no hesitation as he crossed the street and went into the saloon.

It was crowded, but no one was drinking. Harry Randolph had the bar to himself, and he leaned against it, trying to appear nonchalant, but he was keyed to coming trouble. His eyes slid along Willie's bare hip, and he said: "When I came to your town, you bought me a drink, and then I rode out. I'll do the same for you."

"I'll have one," Willie said, and bellied up beside him. He took his drink, pushed the empty glass away from him. A thick silence hung in the room, broken only by heavy breathing and the occasional shuffling of feet.

Kerry said: "You ought to learn to control your impulses a little better. Only little kids can get away with heavin' rocks. Let's go and pay for the windows now."

"Is that the *law?*" Randolph asked.

"No," Willie told him. "That's the decent thing for a man to do."

Randolph looked around the room at his friends. "Coax me a little."

"All right," Willie said, and lashed out with his fist, knocking the man into the ell formed by the bar and the wall. He stepped in quickly, and snatched the gun from the man's waistband, spinning it over his shoulder and away from him. Randolph came erect, and Willie drove the arms down, hitting him on the bridge of the nose with a powerful blow.

Randolph cried out and began to sag, but Kerry supported him as he bent the man's back against the bar. Kerry slapped him viciously, half blinding him.

A man in the crowd cursed, and Kileen's voice came quick and harsh. "Let them alone! Harry wanted it this way!"

Harry Randolph moaned as Kerry hit him again, a dull, popping sound like a stick being slapped in the mud. A man in the crowd groaned sympathetically as Kerry struck him again. It was an efficient beating. When Harry Randolph slid down into the sawdust, Willie emptied a fire bucket of water in his face.

Randolph groaned and sat up.

Willie said: "Let's go pay for the broken windows now."

The man made no attempt to answer or move.

Willie grabbed a handful of his hair, and jerked him to his feet. "Let's go to jail, then," he said, and shoved Randolph toward the front door.

Randolph cursed and tried to fight again, but Willie shoved hard against his chest, and the man fell heavily. Willie stood over him, tall and calm, the star glinting on his shirt front. "I'll lick you again if you insist," Willie told him in a quiet voice that held no temper.

Harry knew that he had lost. He got to his feet, and walked out of the saloon ahead of Kerry.

The merchant was reluctant to place a price on his broken window. He said: "It was all in fun, Sheriff. I'd just as soon let it go."

"Give him ten dollars, then," Willie told Harry.

Randolph pawed the dust with his boot. "What the hell's the fuss about? He said he was satisfied."

Willie glanced at the people watching this from the boardwalk and knew that what he did next might make or break him. He possessed a certain amount of reasonableness, but he had passed it. He ripped Harry's wallet from his pocket, leaving a long strip of cloth dangling. He gave the merchant a ten dollar gold piece, and herded the man across the street to the bakery. This time Randolph paid without additional urging.

Kerry said: "Get this straight . . . I don't give a damn if you break every window in town. I don't care if you wreck the saloon, but whatever you do, you pay for it, either in cash or in jail. No man is free. If you think you are, then fork your horse and get out of here. This town can't use you."

Randolph took this without a flicker coming across his bruised face. He murmured: "I just learned somethin' about you, Kerry. You ain't like Harms at all."

Kileen's crowd layered the saloon porch three deep. They parted to let Randolph through, but none of them followed him inside.

Willie reëntered the hotel, and finished his cold meal. Louise had never left the table during the interruption. She gave him a small smile when he pushed his plate back to roll a smoke.

He said: "You got a lot of confidence . . . sittin' here like that."

"It made a good impression on the crowd," Louise said, and laughed nervously.

Willie noticed that her hands trembled, and he covered them with his own until the trembling stopped.

The girl who had pulled at Randolph's arm came in, and crossed to their table. She said in a small voice: "Can I sit down?"

Willie rose, and handed her into a chair. She was a small girl, barely out of her teens, her body softly molded with the first grace of womanhood.

"What's bothering you?" Kerry asked. "Randolph?"

She folded her hands in her lap and nodded. "Is he in trouble now?"

Willie pulled smoke out of his cigarette, then said: "Randolph just had his trouble. If he wants any more, all he has to do is act big for his britches."

"What's your name?" Louise asked her, and gave her a smile that made instant friends.

"Nanon DeBardon," the girl said. "I . . . that is, Harry and I keep company. Sometimes I worry about him. He and Dillon see a lot of each other."

"Who is Dillon?" Willie asked.

"Kileen's foreman," Nanon said. "He's a mean man, I think. He puts ideas into Harry's head. I think he pushed him tonight." Kileen entered just then, and the girl rose quickly. "I have to go now," she said breathlessly, and hurried out through the back door.

Kileen stopped at Kerry's table. "Can a man sit down?" His eyes followed the girl until she disappeared.

"Help yourself," Kerry invited, and introduced his wife. Kileen laid his hat on the floor, but he was ill at ease.

"Was that a sample of *law* I saw out there?"

"That was justice," Kerry told him. "Sometimes there's a difference. A man answers for what he does . . . drunk or sober. Don't ever forget it."

"Harry did that just to find out what you'd do."

"Then he found out," Willie said. He snuffed out his smoke in his coffee cup. "Kileen, understand something. Harms and I never got along. He was an easy-goin' windbag, for my money. If he'd been out there tonight, he might have laughed it off, if he was in the mood. Maybe tomorrow his mood would be different, and he'd have pistol-whipped Harry. I don't tick that way. What's fair for you is fair for me and the next guy."

165

"We like to settle our own troubles," Kileen stated. "That's where Harms and me never agreed. He wanted to settle everything his way."

Kerry tapped the badge. "This is the law, Kileen, and you better not forget it. If I can't do what's right, then I'll take this thing off and give it to a man that can." He saw no resentment at his words and added: "My wife and I want a house. Know where we can rent one?"

The man leaned back in his chair and gazed wonderingly at Kerry. He lighted a cigar, and puffed until smoke floated around the table, thick and strong. "Kerry," he said, "I just can't figure you out. These people resent your coming here. Can't you see that? They don't want your law. They want to govern themselves."

"From what I've seen," Willie said, "I'm surprised they can blow their own noses."

Kileen waved it aside. "Randolph was just tryin' out his muscles. I mean it, Kerry. These people will resist you with everything they've got. Your missus will have a hard time of it, too."

"I had a horse once," Willie told him. "Pretty thing, but wild as all get out. When that horse got ornery, I pounded the liver out of him. When he behaved himself, then I fed him sugar. Right now that horse and me are the best of friends."

Kileen knew when not to argue. He said: "I never liked that hill bunch, and I'll tell you why. They said we was crazy to come out here . . . maybe we was, but it worked out all right. They wouldn't loan us money or nothin' . . . not even credit at the stores. It was a rough go, I can tell you that, but now we've got it made. We got a bank and our own town, and we hate like hell to be treated like a long lost cousin just because we got a little money." He rose, and picked up his hat.

166

"I'll have a house for you and your missus in the morning. Good night to you."

Louise watched until he went out, then said in a soft voice: "He's a *nice* man, Willie."

They spent the next ten days moving into the new house and cleaning up the grounds. Willie took to lounging on the verandah of the hotel. It afforded him a clean view of the town. By nature he was a man who minded his own business and gave the desert people a chance to mind theirs. He caused a moment's discontent and resentment when he broke up a fight during the Saturday night dance. However, he herded the combatants outside and allowed them to settle it to everyone's satisfaction. In these ten days he had changed hostile stares to brief, curt nods. Louise had gained a speaking foothold with several ladies of the town.

For all of its stiff-backed independence, Willie Kerry found that he liked Morgan Tanks. He found the men to be tough and just, providing they weren't stepped on. He saw Harry Randolph frequently, and the man seemed to hold no grudge, for Kerry's greeting was civilly answered. Once he even paused to talk of the weather and the cattle situation at the railhead.

Another noon found Kerry on the hotel verandah, his feet on the railing and his hat low over his eyes to shut out the glare of the sun. Heat bounced and shimmered from the fawn-colored dust of the street. He turned his head as a rider pounded into town and dismounted by the saloon. Willie watched him go in, then crossed after him a moment later.

Bob Overmile leaned against the bar, and Willie sided him. "Kinda off your feed, ain't you?"

"They found Sam Harms," Overmile said, and cut off his

167

talk until the bartender gave him his beer and moved away.

Willie's voice was cautious. "When and where?"

"Two days ago," Overmile stated. "Dead. Looks like he wandered out on the desert and lost himself. Anyway his canteen was empty. We found his horse about eight miles away . . . picked clean, too."

"Been shot?"

"I guess not," Bob said. "Saber was along, and he couldn't find any bones where a bullet tore through him. It's his guess that Sam was after somebody and got balled up in his own stupidity."

"Any idea who he was after?"

Overmile shrugged. "Buck Dillon, Saber thinks. Buck Kileen's top man. You knew Kileen was havin' trouble?"

"No," Willie said. "I been walkin' like a cat on sparrow eggs. What kinda trouble's Kileen got?"

"Same old stuff," Overmile said. "Some fella named Pickering over on the north edge is gettin' ambitious. Seems that there was already a couple of shots fired, and Dillon fired 'em both. Saber figures that's what Harms went after him for. He didn't want a shootin' war to start." Overmile glanced out the door at the street. "I think I'll start back. This place gives me the creeps."

Kerry waited until he left, then went to the end of the street and got his horse from the stable. He saddled, and rode from town, cutting out on the vast dryness toward Kileen's place. Here the desert was rich and fertile. Irrigation ditches ran a rifle straight course for miles, with branching arms spreading wetness into the land.

Two hours later he sighted the ranch house and didn't check his pace until he came to the edge of the barn. A dull-faced man stepped out of the open doorway and said: "That's as far as any hill sheriff comes around here." He wore a gun in a low holster, and his eyes studied Kerry with an open hostility.

"You're Dillon," Kerry said, crossing his hands on the saddle horn.

"That's right," Dillon agreed. "Now turn that horse and hightail it outta here."

"I knew a fella that was impulsive like you once," Willie said slowly. "A man like that ought not bring his gun to town. He might get riled up and shoot somebody."

A muscle flickered in Dillon's cheek. "I come to town often, and I always carry a gun. It's got to be a habit with me, and I'm a man that don't like to change." Willie gave him no answer, just lifted the reins to move. The man's loud voice halted him. "I told you to get out of here!"

"I heard you," Kerry said, and rapped the horse with his heels.

Buck Dillon had intended to hold his ground, but the plunging roan changed his mind. He leaped aside at the last minute, and Willie rode on up to the ranch house.

Kileen waited on the porch, his eyes humorous and slightly troubled. "Buck will hold that against you, Kerry. He don't like his bluffs to backfire on him that way."

"What's the difference," Willie said. "If it wasn't this, then he'd think up somethin' else. He's that kind." He dismounted, and sat on the porch rail. "What was Harms after Dillon for?"

Kerry laid the question out quickly, but Kileen showed no surprise. It was as if he had been expecting it. He lighted a cigar. "Buck's a wild one, Kerry, but not a dyed-in-the-wool badman. Harms wanted him to lay off Pickering's man before he got a war started, but Buck didn't have any respect for Harms and paid him no mind. Harms went to arrest Buck and got led a merry chase to hell and gone south of here.

That's the last we saw of Harms."

Willie said: "Saber and a bunch found Harms. The heat got him."

Kileen let out a ragged breath. "You know," he said, "I been worried. I thought maybe Buck had shot him."

"What's this beef between you and Pickering?"

"Nothin', actually," Kileen stated. "Pickering's got a hardcase foreman that wants to do a good job. He figures that if he snips off a little of my property and presents it to the boss, then he'll get a pat on the head. Of course, I have the same problem. Buck Dillon wants to show me what a good watchdog he is, and he'll run me into a war if he ain't careful. Sometimes I feel like givin' him his walkin' papers, but then he's a hell of a good man in other respects."

"It's my job to cool this thing off," Kerry said. "Where can I find Pickering?"

"This is Monday," Kileen said. "He comes into Morgan Tanks every Monday night for his supplies and a poker game. Dillon goes in, too . . . sorta hopin' somethin'll happen. He's a persistent cuss."

"Thanks," Willie said. "You've been a big help." He left the porch, then turned and asked: "What made you change your mind about the law, Kileen?"

"I ain't changed it," the rancher replied. "I still want to see my town the county seat of a new county. Howsomever, I have changed my mind about you. There's somethin' outstandin' about you, Kerry."

A flush of pleasure filled Kerry, but he let none of it show in his face. In this straight-laced country, compliments were rare. He nodded and swung up, riding from the yard.

III

He left his house around seven and walked up the darkening street to the center of town. With sundown came a cooling breeze to wash away the searing heat of the day, and Morgan Tanks became a lively little town. Horses stood at the hitch racks, lining the street. Parked buggies added to the jam of traffic. He took his chair on the hotel verandah, and settled down with his feet on the railing.

Nanon DeBardon came out of the mercantile across the street, saw him, and crossed to where he sat. She set her groceries down, and a sudden confusion seemed to grip her.

"What's troubling you?" Kerry asked.

"Harry hasn't been around for three days," Nanon stated. "He's been with Buck Dillon."

"Dillon isn't a criminal," Kerry said. "Harry's a grown man. He has a right to pick his company."

"Dillon's bad for him," Nanon said with some heat. "He puts foolish notions in Harry's head."

Willie took the makings from his shirt pocket, and rolled a smoke. He didn't like advice when it was given to him; in the same breath, he loathed giving it. But the girl was sincere and worried, and it had an effect on the tall, quiet man. "A man's a funny animal," he said. "He'll beat a horse or a dog or even another man because they're bull-headed, but if he wasn't the same way himself, he wouldn't be doin' it. Let's say that I got Harry away from Buck, then what? He'll tie in with the next ringtail that comes along, and you're right back where you started. It's a rough world, Nanon. Let the boy go. If he goes to hell now, then it's better than waitin' until you got three kids. He'll either come out of it, or he won't. Poundin' a man over the head with his lessons is no good. Experience is a crazy teacher . . . you get the experience first, and the lessons afterward."

"Men are so coldly logical," Nanon said.

"Nope," Willie contradicted. "They want to bawl and raise hell just like a woman, but they don't. They got a lot of false pride that a woman ain't got. When it comes down to makin' a practical bargain, you can't beat a woman."

Nanon kneaded her hands. "If your wife's at home . . . I wondered if she'd mind my talking to her."

"She'd be delighted," Willie said, and watched Nanon scurry down the street.

He idled an hour away, then lifted his head as Harry Randolph came out of the saloon, and stood for a moment on the porch.

The man fastened his eyes on Kerry, then came to a decision, and crossed the dust. Randolph sat on the porch rail, facing the sheriff, and said: "I hear you and Buck had words."

"He did most of the talking," Kerry admitted. He noticed that the young man wore no gun.

"Dillon'll wear his gun tonight," Randolph stated. "He's that kind."

"And I'll take it away from him," Kerry said. "I'm *that* kind."

Interest rose in Randolph's eyes. "This might be worth seeing. Dillon's no plum, Sheriff."

"My observation," Willie said, "is that a man'll go around makin' threats 'cause he's tryin' to prove something. Usually he's tryin' to prove he's tough . . . not to anyone else, but to himself."

"You got an answer to everything, ain't you?"

"Yep," Kerry admitted, "and usually the wrong one." He stopped talking as Dillon rode in from the east. He gave Kerry a bold glance in passing, and pulled in before the hitch rack across the street. He wore his gun low against his thigh and shifted it as he dismounted. Dillon gave the sheriff another quick look, then opened the doors of the saloon, drawing his gun at the same time.

Sound bucketed up and down the street, rolling over the town as he announced his arrival with a shot into the ceiling. Kerry left the porch unhurriedly and crossed the dust. Randolph followed three paces behind him. Townspeople filled the boardwalk, and Kerry understood that word had gone around.

The saloon was crowded with noise and men. The gun coughed again, followed by the *tinkle* of splintered glass. Kerry stepped in the door as Dillon shattered another bottle with his .44 Colt. The man gave Kerry a brazen grin and said: "Well, well, the sheriff. I was just havin' a little fun. You don't mind me havin' fun, do you?"

Willie narrowed the distance with each step. "I guess your hearin' was outta whack the other day." His voice was low and cool, and it wiped the grin from Buck Dillon's face.

Dillon shifted the gun, pointing it at Kerry's middle. "Hold it where you are! I guess you're one of them crazy men that ain't got sense enough to know when a man means somethin'."

Willie halted three feet away from the man. He raised a hand easily and shoved his hat to the back of his head. "Hell," he said mildly, "we can talk this over, can't we?"

Dillon grinned then, and he let out a relieved breath. Willie whipped off his hat, and slapped the man across the face with the stiff brim. The gun went off, gouging out a long splinter from the floor, and Dillon staggered blindly. Willie clubbed a forearm down across the gun hand, sending the weapon to the floor with a sharp clatter.

He hit Dillon with a doubled fist, driving him back against

173

his friends, and following to sledge him again. Dillon went to his knees, still half blinded and numb from the blows. Kerry placed his hat back on his head, and tugged it at the proper angle.

Dillon was getting his eyes to focus again when Kerry stepped into him. The man tried to put up a fight, but Willie kept hitting him before he could set himself. Dillon bled freely from the nose and mouth. Kerry pounded him flat, and the man stayed there. Willie picked up the fallen gun, and dropped it into a spittoon, then hoisted Dillon to his shoulder, and left the saloon.

Men poured out of the building, and followed him to the small jail. He locked the groaning man in one of the small cells, and closed the outside door. Harry Randolph eyed Kerry when he stepped to the boardwalk. The man grinned and rubbed his jaw. "Know just how Buck feels," he said, and turned, shoving his way through the crowd.

Men stood in silence, but the sheriff saw that it wasn't sullen. It gave him some encouragement. He said: "From now on there won't be any guns worn in Morgan Tanks. Leave them at some business place when you come to town. Pick 'em up on the way out."

A man in the front row muttered: "Hell."

Willie focused his attention on him. "You wear one and see what happens."

"I just saw," the man said. That broke up the gathering.

Inside the jail, Buck Dillon regained his senses and pounded against the barred door, shouting in a wild, high voice. Willie reëntered and asked: "What's got you by the tail?"

"Damn you!" Dillon said. "You let me outta here damn' quick!"

"I told you something," Kerry said, "and you didn't have

enough sense to believe it. You gotta learn you ain't the only sparrow on the roost."

"I'll kill you for this," Dillon threatened.

Willie shook his head. "You just cool off a little while. If you behave yourself, I'll let you out when I come back. If you can't, then jail's the place for you." He grinned when Dillon cursed, then went out, and crossed to the hotel.

He found Pickering in the lobby, a tall, gaunt man with a shock of white hair. Willie introduced himself and said: "Pickering, if your foreman's in town, then find him and tell him there's to be no trouble tonight."

The man looked Kerry over carefully. "He's across the street at the mercantile. If you want to talk to him, his name's Wilder." There was no obstinacy in Pickering, just reserve. He placed the sheriff on his own, letting him run his course without help or interference.

"Thanks," Kerry said, and went back across the street.

Wilder was a big man with a wide, sun-blackened face and large hairy hands. He wore a gun high on his hip, and Kerry walked up to him unnoticed and slipped it from his holster. He threw it through an open door leading into a back room.

Wilder spun around, his temper high.

"There's a new rule," Willie told him. "No guns in town."

There was nothing impetuous about Wilder. He wanted to be sure before he acted. "Who's gonna make this rule stick?"

"I just made it stick," Willie said. "I made it stick with Buck Dillon, too."

Wilder possessed a deep temper that he didn't allow to reach the surface. It only edged its way into his voice. "Give me another gun, Amos." He spoke to the clerk, but never took his eyes from Kerry's face.

A glass showcase door whispered as it slid open, and Kerry said in a soft voice: "No gun, Amos."

There was a heartbeat of silence, then Amos Wilkerson said testily: "I'll sell to who I damn' please."

"All right," Kerry stated. "Wrap it up and he can take it with him when he leaves town." He waited with this thing pushing against him, ugly and wild and slightly dangerous.

Wilder broke the spell when he let out his breath and wheeled away from the counter, then plunged from the store.

Amos sighed with relief. "You just ain't like Harms at all, Kerry." Wilkerson's voice contained a faint friendliness, and it halted Kerry.

"What really happened between Dillon and Wilder?"

"Dillon wants a fight . . . so does Wilder."

"Why don't they fight, then, and get it over with?" Kerry wanted to know.

"I guess 'cause there ain't no excuse," Amos stated. "Wilder's a cautious man. He don't buy trouble . . . never did, but he can't stand for no pushin' around. Dillon'd like to pull his gun, but he's looking for a legal excuse, like an open war between Pickering and Kileen."

"I thought Wilder pushed first," Kerry said.

"I heard that, too," Amos agreed, "but I discount it . . . mainly because I got it from Dillon."

"Thanks for the talk," Kerry told him, and left the store.

Pickering and Wilder were in the hotel lobby when he entered. He crossed to them and got right to the point. "This squabble between you and Buck Dillon is gonna get settled tonight . . . once and for all. I'm gonna let him outta jail in a little while."

"I got no gun," Wilder said.

"What makes you think you'll need one?"

"Why . . . the man threatened me," Wilder said. He shot a glance at Pickering who kept his eyes lowered and studied his fingers. Pickering was the kind of a man who gave the other man all the rope he wanted, content to sit back and watch human nature run its course. Kerry was shouldering the responsibility of his troubles by forcing the issue, and Pickering was willing to let it go at that.

"Dillon don't have a gun, either," Willie stated. "If there's anything between you that needs settling, then do it with fists or beer bottles, but not guns."

"You walk pretty proud," Wilder said. "I've known men to get into real trouble walkin' like that."

"I bought real trouble when I put on this badge," Willie told him. "Before the night's over, you two fightin' cocks are gonna learn to walk on the same side of the street without lockin' horns."

Pickering had remained neutral up to this point. Now he raised his head and said: "Kerry, I haven't made up my mind if you're a damn' fool or a great man. You seem to forget that men will fight. Sometimes even God can't keep 'em apart."

"Fightin's all right," Willie said. "Killin' ain't."

He went out onto the porch to resume his seat. He waited until Pickering and his foreman crossed to the saloon, then rose and went over to the jail.

He opened the door for Dillon. The man's face was swollen and caked with dried blood. He glared at Kerry for a long moment, before he said: "What is this? First you lock me up, then you turn me loose. Are you trying to play it big for the people's benefit?"

"Get out of here," Willie said. "Pickering and Wilder are both in town, and neither of them is armed. If you want to fight Wilder, then do it with your fists. Do it tonight or leave him alone."

"Don't tell me how to fight, or when," Dillon snapped. "I'll settle with Wilder, then I'll come after you."

177

"That would be a foolish thing," Willie said.

He stood in the doorway after Dillon went out, deeply in thought, then blew out the lamp, and walked to his house on the back street.

Lamplight blossomed in the parlor, and Willie paused in the archway. Louise was serving coffee to three townswomen. She rose, knowing instinctively that something troubled the tall man. She excused herself, and followed Willie into their bedroom.

He took his gun and holster from the dresser drawer, and buckled them on. Louise's eyebrows pulled together in a small frown, and she spoke in a low voice. "Trouble?"

"Maybe," Willie said. "I don't know yet." He wished she wouldn't watch him with such steadiness. He raised his head quickly. "You think it's wrong . . . this gun?"

"I wouldn't say, Willie. You have to decide for yourself."

Willie blew out a long breath. "I'm not a brave man . . . I never claimed to be. I been playin' this thing without a gun, but now I got doubts. Somehow I need this gun."

Louise came to him, and laid her head against his chest. "You do what you think is right, Willie. That makes it right with me."

He turned from her, and went back uptown.

The long-barreled .44 was a strange weight against his thigh as he resumed his station on the hotel verandah. He watched Kileen wheel into town. The man saw Kerry and crossed to him.

Kileen said: "I see you're wearin' a gun tonight. It looks a little strange on you, Kerry."

"I feel worse for it," Kerry admitted, studying the movement along the street.

Kileen caught the sheriff's shifting attention and asked: "Dillon and Wilder tangle yet?"

"No," Willie said, and told him of his trouble with Dillon.

Kileen twisted his mouth to one side and scrubbed the back of his neck with his hand. "Well, you been runnin' your business and lettin' us run ours. I don't mean to advise you, but Dillon won't forget that. If Wilder don't plug him, then he'll come after you."

"Wilder won't shoot him," Kerry stated. "He doesn't have a gun, and he's man enough not to get one."

Kileen grunted. "Maybe you're right. He ain't a proddy man when it comes right down to it." He slapped his flat belly and stated: "Come on and have a drink with me."

"I'm a hill man," Kerry reminded him, and waited for the reaction.

Kileen shrugged. "Tonight I don't feel like drawin' a line on where a man's from."

Kerry grinned, and they walked across the street to the saloon.

Pickering and Wilder left their table to join them at the bar.

Willie tossed off his drink and folded his hands. "Pickering," he said, "what you got against the *law?*"

"Nothin'," the gaunt man said. "I didn't like Harms or any of his deppities, that's all."

"Law's a queer thing," Kileen philosophized. "A man can't live among other men without it, but it's gotta be tempered a little with judgment. Harms didn't have any judgment, and without that there ain't no justice, either."

Kerry said: "You oughta know by now that you and me ain't much different in the way we think. When I get back to Hondo, I'll see Saber, and maybe we can split the county. It'll take time, maybe years, but it'll give you common ground for talk."

Pickering and Kileen nodded in agreement, then Kileen

touched Wilder and asked: "You seen Dillon yet?"

"He went past twenty minutes ago with Randolph, but he just glared."

"May be a quiet night, after all," Pickering said.

They ordered a round of beer and settled against the bar in small conversation until the wall clock indicated nine-thirty. Kerry was ready to go back to the hotel when Harry Randolph came in. He said to the sheriff: "Buck Dillon's got hold of a gun."

"What have you got to do with it?" Kerry wanted to know.

"I don't want nothin' to do with it," Randolph insisted. "You can believe what you damn' please, but I tried to talk some sense into him. He won't listen to nobody. He's out on the street now."

"I knew this couldn't last," Kileen said, and drained his beer. "I pay his wages . . . I'll go out and talk to him." He left the saloon.

"Nanon worries about you," Kerry said to Randolph.

"Dammit, I know it!"

"You gotta show her she ain't got nothin' to worry about," Kerry said.

"What you expect me to do?"

"The right thing," Kerry said. "Whatever comes natural." He looked past Randolph's shoulder as Kileen came back in.

"It's dark out there," Randolph said. "If Wilder shows himself, Dillon will think he's armed. The man needs a gun to make him feel big. He thinks everyone else's the same way."

The young man's talk ate into Kerry, and he knew then why he was wearing a gun. He took it off and handed it to the bartender. "Keep this for me until I call for it."

Pickering took him by the arm and said stiffly: "This is

goin' too far. Put that damn' thing back on.''

"I said, no guns in town, and I mean it. What applies to him applies to me. It'll be better this way.'' He shook the man's hand off, and stepped out onto the porch, and Pickering and Kileen followed him.

Dillon drew his gun when the sheriff made the center of the street. "Don't come any closer!'' he yelled.

Willie closed the distance with three more steps.

"Trigger that thing off,'' he said, "and you'll never know another day's peace in your life. You can only kill a man, Dillon. The badge never dies. It's just pinned to the shirt of another man and keeps coming after you until you're swingin' from a tree.''

"I want Wilder!'' Dillon shouted.

When he was six feet away from the man, Willie knew that Dillon would never let him get any closer. He sensed the tightening of the man's trigger finger and leaped aside and into him as the gun spit fire and noise.

He struck the arm down just in time, and drove Dillon into the hitch rack, letting the weight and momentum of his charge arch the man's back. Dillon cried out as Kerry grasped his wrist and twisted, spinning the gun into the dust.

Dillon's rage vaulted, and he fought to free himself, but Willie slammed him along the jaw with an elbow and threw him headlong into the street with a violent twist of his body. He leaped astride when Dillon tried to rise, placing his knee in the man's neck until his face changed color and his fight grew weak.

Randolph and the crowd gathered in a tight ring around them. Willie stood up, leaving the man gagging for wind. He took Randolph roughly by the arm and handed him a small ring of keys. "Go lock this damn' troublemaker up.''

"That suits me just dandy,'' Randolph said, and jerked

Dillon to his feet. Dillon tried to put up a fight, but Randolph slapped him quiet.

The man stood sawing for wind. Some of the wildness faded from his eyes when he looked at Kerry. "Damn," he muttered, "but you and Harms is sure different."

Pickering broke up the crowd with his rough voice, and they crossed to the verandah of the hotel. Wilder leaned against the wall. Kileen sagged into a chair and lighted a cigar. Willie felt the aftermath of the fight work through him, and leaned his hands on the porch rail to steady the trembling.

Kileen saw this and said, not unkindly: "So you ain't all nerve, after all?"

"No," Kerry admitted. "Just human and scared sometimes."

"You figure to leave Randolph on here as your deppity?" Pickering asked.

"Can't he handle it?" Willie asked.

The gaunt man nodded.

Kerry turned his head to look beyond the town and onto the flatness of the desert. The moon stood high, sending a pale white light onto it, giving it a beauty and wildness that was not frightening. Looking at it from Hondo, it had always seemed different, shimmering in the distance, but tonight, from the hotel porch, it looked familiar and friendly, and he was glad that he had come to know it.

About the Author

Will Cook is the author of numerous outstanding Western novels as well as historical frontier fiction. He was born in Richmond, Indiana, but was raised by an aunt and uncle in Cambridge, Illinois. He joined the U.S. Cavalry at the age of sixteen but was disillusioned because horses were being eliminated through mechanization. He transferred to the U.S. Army Air Force in which he served in the South Pacific during the Second World War. Cook turned to writing in 1951 and contributed a number of outstanding short stories to *Dime Western* and other pulp magazines as well as fiction for major smooth-paper magazines such as *The Saturday Evening Post*. It was in the *Post* that his best-known novel, *Comanche Captives*, was serialized. It was later filmed as *Two Rode Together* (Columbia, 1961) directed by John Ford and starring James Stewart and Richard Widmark. It has now been restored, as was the author's intention, and comprises part of the three volumes in *A Saga of Texas* published by Five Star Westerns. Sometimes in his short stories Cook would introduce characters that would later be featured in novels, such as Charlie Boomhauer who first appeared in "Lawmen Die Sudden" in *Big-Book Western* in 1953 and is later to be found in *Badman's Holiday* (1958) and *The Wind River Kid* (1958). Along with his steady productivity, Cook maintained an enviable quality. His novels range widely in time and place, from the

Illinois frontier of 1811 to southwest Texas in 1905, but each is peopled with credible and interesting characters whose interactions form the backbone of the narrative. Indeed, his fiction is known for its strong heroines. Another common feature is Cook's compassion for his characters that must be able to survive in a wild and violent land. His protagonists make mistakes, hurt people they care for, and sometimes succumb to ignoble impulses, but this all provides an added dimension to the artistry of his work.

ABOUT THE EDITOR

Bill Pronzini was born in Petaluma, California. His earliest Western fiction was published under his own name and a variety of pseudonyms in *Zane Grey Western Magazine*. Among his most notable Western novels are *Starvation Camp* (1984) and *Firewind* (1989). He is also the editor of numerous Western story collections, including *Under the Burning Sun: Western Stories* (Five Star Westerns, 1997) by H. A. DeRosso, *Renegade River: Western Stories* (Five Star Westerns, 1998) by Giff Cheshire, and *Tracks in the Sand* by H. A. DeRosso (2001), among others. His own Western story collection, *All the Long Years* (Five Star Westerns, 2001), has recently been published. His next Five Star Western will be *Burgade's Crossing*.

The employees of Five Star hope you have enjoyed this book. All our books are made to last. Other Five Star books are available at your library, through selected bookstores, or directly from us.

For information about titles, please call:

(800) 223-1244

or visit our web site at:

www.gale.com/fivestar

To share your comments, please write:

Publisher
Five Star
295 Kennedy Memorial Drive
Waterville, ME   04901